The Price of Obsession

A Novel

By Natalie Tina Martin

Part One

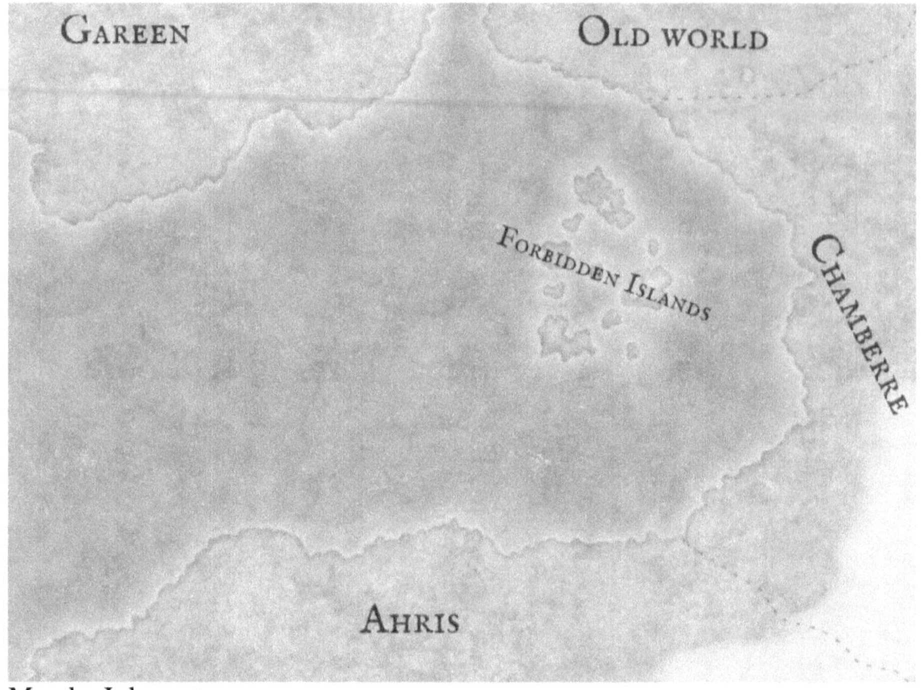

Map by Inkarnate

Acknowledgements

This has been a labor of love and tears, and there are so many people I want to thank. First my husband, my editor, Frank Kaminski, who helped support my dream of being a writer. I also need to thank my closest and dearest friends, Alyssa, Barbara, and Ginger, who have always supported me throughout all my endeavors. I must also thank my beta readers, Ivy and Vicky, whose insights were invaluable.

ISBN-979-8-3232334-3-4

Printed in the United States

Chapter 1

It was a crypt. Dank, dark, with a stench so foul it made one wish for death's ever-looming presence to just take them. The stone walls blanketed them in darkness and drowned out their screams. The chains rattled as Merrin shifted his arms, his deeply scarred wrists having calloused over the years. His thoughts drifted for just a moment to the sweet smile of his wife and the laughter of his children. This idyllic scene was quickly shattered by another memory: that of the Lord standing over his pregnant wife, her eye black and lip swollen as he undid his trousers. Rage filled him as it had on that day. Cursing, he jerked hard on the chains, testing them to no avail.

"Settle down, Merrin," the familiar old voice called out to him in the dark. "Don't give the guards any more reason to come after you."

"Perhaps they could just end it quickly then," Merrin sighed, leaning back against the cold wet stone. "Death is preferable to this."

"I told you I would help you and I shall. I just need for you to be patient." Sephtis reached out in the dark and patted the other man's arm. They had been cellmates ever since Sephtis had been thrown down here, though Sephtis's sentence was far shorter: a mere six months, whereas Merrin had been here for two years.

Merrin sighed and bowed his head forward. "How can you help me, Sephtis? I'm in here for murder. Despite it being justified."

"Yes, but I have my ways." Sephtis heard the grating sound of iron keys being stuffed into a lock, followed by the familiar click of the key being turned, which sent both prisoners' ears on high alert. One never knew what was going to happen: food, a beating, time outside, news from family—or, if one were still new and dared to hope...freedom.

"The guards are coming," shushed Sephtis. The two prisoners listened intently to the approaching footsteps and tensed as their sound abruptly halted right outside the cell. There was the familiar jangle of keys as the guards unlocked the cell door. One of the guards carried a torch that bathed the prisoners in blinding light, forcing them to squint in pain.

"Get up, old man," one of the guards barked as he walked toward Sephtis. His steel armor was polished to a high gleam. It was obvious he had never seen any real battle. Sephtis started to stand, his bare feet having grown accustomed to the prick of the straw they threw down at them to serve as their bedding. They treated them worse than the animals in the sheds outside. The guard began undoing Sephtis's shackles. "Your time is up," the soldier growled. Growling seemed the only way these soldiers knew how to communicate with prisoners. Or yelling—that was another way.

"Good for you, Sephtis," Merrin sighed, happy that his friend was getting out. That man was the only reason he'd stayed alive for as long as he had.

"Shut up." A swift kick to Merrin's ribs made him hiss in pain. He'd already had one beating this week, but the noble family of the man he'd killed paid extra for added punishment.

"Leave him be!" Sephtis snapped once the shackles were off. The one-time healer bent down to use what little bit of magic he had left to heal his friend.

"I wouldn't bother," exulted the soldier. "I also came down to tell you, Merrin..." He spat his name out with disgust. "...that your wife died and is being buried tomorrow and your children were sent to the orphanage." The soldier laughed as he grabbed Sephtis and began dragging him out.

"Remember what I said, Merrin! Do not give up!" Sephtis shouted as he was marched up the stairs. When the doors to the vestibule opened and he got his first breath of fresh air, Sephtis felt tears of joy. The soldiers led him the rest of the way to the front doors and then forcefully pushed him through. As he raised his pale hands to shield his eyes from the sun, a familiar figure suddenly moved in front of him.

"So you're out, finally," said the gravelly voice of a tall dark-haired man with gray-green eyes, holding a package filled with new clothes. "I don't know why you didn't just have *her* break you out. Come on, you smell awful." He wrapped his strong arm around the old man and began helping him down the road.

"You try living in a cell for six months and see if you come up smelling like roses," Sephtis retorted. "Where is she, anyway?" Sephtis glanced around for her and frowned.

"Where she always is: working her magic to relieve nobles of their wealth," Finnegan chuckled. "She wanted to be here but she was about to bag a wealthy one. She figured you would understand since it was going to help pay the crew for waiting around."

"I should have brought more funds..." Sephtis rubbed his beard. "So is that what you two have been up to while I've been incarcerated?" Sephtis snorted and shook his head when a sly smile spread across his dirt- and dust-covered lips. "Tell her I need her to get caught by the guards. She will be breaking out my friend Merrin."

"It seems a bit dangerous on such short notice," Finnegan replied slowly. He hated sending her into danger without someone there to back her up in case things went wrong.

"Are you doubting her ability?" Sephtis asked, feeling his strength slowly return as his magic began to blossom inside of him. The prison from which he'd just been freed was a place designed to suppress magic, with wards inscribed on its walls to prevent mages from building their power, and shackles used to siphon their magical energy. But he was a powerful mage and could at least use the little magic he had left to help Merrin survive.

"Of course not, but you know she won't like it, and who knows what those bastards will do to her if they catch her..." Finnegan sighed. "So what do you wish me to do?" There was no point in arguing. The old man always got his way.

"I need her to get him out and deliver him to the island. I need you to find his wife's body so I can prepare her for the ritual. Her name is Penelope Blackmoore. She recently passed, so it shouldn't be too hard." Sephtis paused to take a deep breath.

"Isn't that what got you in trouble last time, grave robbing?" Finnegan paused, waiting for Sephtis to move again.

"That was because I'm an old man. You are spry and quick. If trouble comes, you can get away. Though I doubt there will be any. She was disowned by her family for marrying Merrin. She will be in a pauper's grave. But still keep wary; we don't need K trying to get both of you out of jail." The old man chuckled and continued walking.

"Wait, did you say Merrin Blackmoor? The Merrin Blackmoor who killed a noble who tried to rape his wife?" Finnegan asked, looking down at Sephtis.

"Yes. He never deserved his fate. Rotten politics. He tried to look out for me in there and in the end I looked out for him. He is a good friend. I will not leave him to his fate." Sephtis shook his head, letting go of a deep sigh. "So much work to be done."

"Well, you will have plenty of time to figure it all out. Right now let's get you a room, a bath, and some food. I have just the place. It's nothing fancy but it's clean." Finnegan led Sephtis to the poorer side of town. The cobblestone streets gave way to dirt and the neighborhood's own strange aroma. It was a mixture of food, garbage, and a few other unappealing smells that kept the upper class away.

The Dansbry, despite its humble appearance, was a decent establishment. The proprietor did his best to keep things clean and organized. He never asked questions and never gave out any information. Finnegan opened the door and nodded at the man behind the counter, who merely pointed to the rooms in back. Finnegan got to the backroom, found an open door, and placed Sephtis inside on a worn old chair. "Take it easy for a minute. I'll have them to prepare a bath for you and get you some food. I brought you your robes and a couple potions K said you would want to drink once you got settled." Finnegan arranged everything neatly on the worn table.

After his stay in the dungeon, Sephtis felt as if he were now in paradise. Behind a wall screen was a well-used wooden tub with clean but stained towels that lay folded upon a rickety stool. The bed was simply made from wood, leather, and straw, with a sheet over the top. But Sephtis didn't care. Finnegan set the weakened old man on the bed.

"I'll get water and dinner for you." He saw the certain look in the old man's eyes and immediately knew what it meant. He'd been employed by him long enough to read him.

"Good, good," Sephtis muttered, his mind whirling. It felt so good to lie on something soft. The pain of the hay poking him didn't even faze him.

Moments later a few servants began to fill the old tub with steaming hot water. Sephtis didn't even wait. Tearing off his rags, he crawled into the water and sighed with happiness. The filth began to wash away. He took the soap and began scrubbing himself with it, not even caring that it smelled like flowers.

Once he was sure he had scrubbed every part of his body, he got out and dried himself off, rubbing furiously to make his blood run faster. Wrapping the towel around his waist, Septhis eagerly unwrapped the package Finnegan had left for him, carefully peeling off the layers of brown paper and twine.

Inside lay blue robes of the finest material—heavy velvet, silk, and gold embroidery. Putting the pieces on and finally tying the sash, he let out a breath. He was himself again. He smirked gazing into the mirror. Well, sort of himself; he still needed to shave.

"Sir, we have dinner for you," a voice called from the door to his room.

"Come in," he called, eager to eat anything besides bread and water.

The maid stepped in carrying a large tray, on which sat roast chicken, potatoes, and even some vegetables. Finnegan must have paid a pretty penny for this feast. There was even a bottle of wine.

The older woman placed the tray on the table and set everything up for him. "Is there anything else I can get you?" Her voice was kind but tired and Sephtis only smiled. "No, you have a good night."

"Thank you." She gave him a half smile and left him alone in the room.

Sephtis sat down. He knew he shouldn't eat too much after years of barely anything, but he still dove into his food, moaning audibly in delight. A part of him did feel guilty—Merrin was probably in agony. Taking a drink of wine, he frowned for a moment. "Don't worry, Merrin, I will take care of her...and I will take care of you."

His attention turned to the door as he heard it creak open. He saw Finnegan step through and into the room. "Well, you look and smell a lot better," he said. "Don't eat too much. I don't want to clean up puke." The pirate sauntered over to the table and took the empty chair, spinning it before sitting down.

Sephtis grunted but pushed the food back and wiped his mouth before sighing. "There is no need to watch over me, Finnegan. I will drink my potions and rest upon this bed. You, though, have matters to attend to—mainly K. I will find you in the morning."

"Get some sleep, old man. I'll take care of everything," Finnegan chuckled, helping the mage to the bed.

"You're a good lad, Finnegan," Sephtis muttered while wrapping the blanket around him and sighing contentedly.

"Ha ha, only because you pay me so well," Finnegan teased and left the room, shutting the door quietly. *And because you owe me.* He breathed in and then let out a long heavy sigh. K would not be pleased with this new plan. Nope. But it's not like she had a choice.

Chapter 2

Shoving his calloused hands into his pockets, Finnegan began whistling low as he headed toward the swanky inn where K was staying. Ladies made eyes at him as he passed by and he winked in return, making them blush and fan themselves profusely. He couldn't help but chuckle.

The large inn began to appear as Finnegan left the old part of town and entered the newer, fancier...richer part. Rarely did he come to this side unless he needed something from the higher-end stores.

He still got looks from the ladies but there was a hint of scorn, too. For all the pride he took in maintaining a neat, clean appearance, he still looked like a renegade in these bougier parts. With his usual swaggering gait he entered the inn and spotted K leaning against the staircase. She fully looked the part of the snotty noble, blending in so well with those around her that had Finnegan not recognized her brown wig and black hat—trademarks of a character he knew so well—he would have missed her.

"Hello, lovely K," Finnegan purred as he sauntered over to her.

"Damn it, Finnegan, I'm working." K's currently blue eyes looked up at him.

"I know, but Sephtis has new orders. He wants you to get caught and bust out a certain Merrin Blackmoor." His eyes darted for a moment as he looked around to make sure no one had heard him.

"What?!" Her cheeks flushed red and her eyes flashed angrily, but she quickly regained her composure. Glancing around, K fanned herself and placed a perfect smile on her face. "Is he insane?" she growled through gritted teeth.

"What, you can't do it?" How Finnegan enjoyed goading her.

"Screw you, Finnegan," K sighed as she rolled her eyes. "I can get him out; it's just short notice, damn it. What do I do with him?"

"You have to disguise him and get him to the island. We are heading there in a few days." Finnegan pulled on one of her curls and she batted his hand away.

"Fine. It's going to take time and it's not going to be easy." Shifting her weight, K looked around. "All right, head back to him and tell him it will be done. But I need money left in the usual spot so I can escape with him."

"Hopefully he still has money left," Finnegan muttered, then grinned. "I know you will have fun, K. Just admit it."

"Yeah, yeah...well, damn...my mark is gone... Now shoo, Finnegan." K gave a slight smile to the pirate. "I'll see you back home."

Unable to resist one last tease, Finnegan added, "Oh, and apparently this Merrin is a rather handsome lad. Not sure if he's as handsome as me, though." Finnegan winked at her and headed off to begin his search for Mrs. Blackmoor.

There was no question what Sephtis had planned. But Finnegan did wonder if Sephtis was doing this out of the kindness of his heart for a friend—or out of his own obsession. He shrugged and, suspecting he might find Mrs. Blackmoor in a gathering place for the less fortunate, headed to the first poor church he could find to begin his search.

Meanwhile K sighed indignantly as she watched her mark slip away. He would have made her so much money...money she could definitely use. She had planned to use some of it to pay the sailors, but now she would have to look elsewhere for their payment. She knew that Sephtis had a stash of money, but she had no idea where it was, not having had the chance to ask him while he was in prison. She also needed money to update her fashion: looks were beginning to change and she needed to keep up. But Sephtis got what Sephtis wanted. There was no way she would go to prison in the middle of a heist; she would always be on their books. No, it needed to be something else, something that would let her scout the prison without catching any attention. As she tapped her fingers on the banister, her eyes lit up. She knew exactly what to do. This was no easy task that the damn crazy mage wanted.

Heading up the stairs to her room, K shed her stifling noble garb and eased into an old woolen coat. Cramming her disguise into her messenger bag, she wrapped it around her body, headed to the large window, and popped the gold latch. The stars were bright but the moon was barely visible. The cool air made her breath curl and wisp in front of her. Using a chair, she climbed up and slipped out the window. She ran across the rooftop, her leather boots muffling any sounds as her nimble feet glided over the shingles.

Tucked away in the far corner of the beyond-poor side of town was a little shanty that K called her own. Dropping down in front of the entrance, she undid several locks and headed inside. She'd had a few years to set up home as it were. The one-room building held racks of clothing, shoes, and hats, and the walls were lined with various weapons and anything she would need to accessorize who she was at any given time. On the right were a large fire pit, a cauldron, a table, and a cupboard for food preparation. In the middle was a small round dining table with a few worn chairs. There was one ornate chair with green velvet next to a small table with a mirror. Toward the left was a large bed filled with feather blankets, pillows, and luxurious sheets. It wasn't much, but it was hers.

K scanned the various racks before deciding on a poor woman's dress and shoes. She quickly stripped out of her breeches. She brought out a brooch that looked like a starburst, one with lock picks for rays. These golden picks would ensure that any lock that dared put up a fuss would be quickly dealt with. Looking through her scarves she found a red plaid one and pinned the brooch to it. This was her character's only precious possession, a family heirloom passed down from mother to daughter.

There were several wigs to choose from and the one she picked was a blond one done up in a bun. Looking around the room, she grabbed her herb basket and added her knife. She might as well keep an eye out, and it was a great excuse as to why she was out at night. She made her way back outside, making sure to lock all her doors again.

No one noticed her as she wandered the streets scoping out various possible escape routes from the prison. As she walked closer she gauged how many soldiers were outside. Making her way around the building she saw a few men posted on each of the prison's four corners. Most of them ignored her. Every once in a while one would make a joke out of boredom. They kept a wary eye out but walked with no real sense of urgency. They just stuck to their patrol route. When they spotted her, she told them she was gathering herbs for potions and they just shooed her away.

The prison was built at the edge of the bay. The night moon was just a sliver, giving K all the coverage she needed to get behind the prison. Gritting her teeth, she slipped into the cold salty water, which was a bit reinvigorating in a wanting-to-run-out-screaming type of way. At least it was keeping her awake, though the salt was beginning to make her skin itch as she began making her way around the prison's edge.

"There has to be a way out..." she muttered to herself, her teeth starting to chatter as the seawater began to seep its way up her clothing. Hearing a guard, she pressed herself closer to the wall and sank deeper into the water. Once the guard's footsteps could no longer be heard on the battlement above, K stood up and kept trudging through the water around the walls. Finally she spotted the gate that led to a tunnel. It was rusted and looked like it led to the sewer portion of the prison. The only question was where did it start. If she was lucky, this was a grate where they tossed all their rubbish and filth to get washed away with the tides.

Heading slowly over to it, she pulled out her picks and began working her magic. Her deft hands made short work of the task. She left the lock open, but only barely so—the guards may be lazy, but there was no point in taking any risks. Looking over the prison and surrounding scenery one more time, she marked the grate's location in her mind. She then began to trudge, then swim, to gauge the distance between this grate and the long-abandoned warship that had been brought in from the tide during a particularly nasty war at sea. It was the stern that had washed up, its underside covered in barnacles. Broken pieces of the mast were scattered around. It was intact enough to get inside, though doing so would be a bit dangerous.

The wood had rotted over the years due to the constant battering of seawater against it. It looked natural as it lay in the beach's white sands, perhaps because it blended in so well with the forest that bordered the coastline. The stark greens, yellows, and browns of nearby overhanging trees shaded the old bones.

The plan was starting to formulate in K's head, and as she mulled it over, she gave into the desire to head home and take a hot bath.

Chapter 3

Standing in her small clothes, K curled her petite toes and padded softly over to the bed, which was rather luxurious for such a dive house. Toweling off her hair until it was only slightly damp, she tossed the towel and began crawling into bed, thinking about what her next move would be.

There was a knock on the door and her hand slid to the knife underneath her pillow.

"It's me," Finnegan's voice echoed.

Sighing, she got up, headed to the door, undid all the locks, and opened the door with a rough jerk. "What is it?" K glared at him, but her expression softened when she saw the look on his face. She knew that look, and it meant he was lonely and needed her company.

Finnegan grinned at her. "You are such a sexy minx, you know that?"

"Shut up," K laughed. As much as Finnegan flirted with her, his heart belonged to a bonnie lass named Nora. Nora had been kidnapped a few years ago and Finnegan had been looking for her ever since. Sephtis was the one who had found the trail and he'd been close to finding her when he'd been caught and sent to jail. Looking at Finnegan, she relented and stepped back to admit him. He dropped his jacket and kicked off his boots.

"So what have you been doing?" K asked, crawling back into bed, followed moments later by Finnegan.

"I had to find where Mrs. Blackmoor was being buried. I just got done telling Sephtis. He's preparing his elixir as we speak and I am to unbury her tomorrow night." He grabbed one of the several pillows and shoved it under his head, then rolled onto his side facing her. "How is your adventure going?"

"I think it's time for Aunt Clara to make an appearance," K murmured as she settled into soft pillows.

"Oh... I like Aunt Clara... She can be such a feisty woman." It didn't take long for both of them to fall fast asleep.

When the morning light streamed into her small hovel, K blinked and groaned. *Gods, I hate mornings.* Grumbling and crawling out from under the covers, she let out a massive sigh and rubbed her face. Finnegan had left long ago to run errands for Sephtis.

With a grunt, she tossed the heavy feather blanket and gingerly stepped onto the cold floor. *A rug—that's also what I would have gotten with the money, Sephtis.* K forced herself upright and began to get ready. Creating today's identity, Aunt Clara, took time and lots of patience. Clearing the table of yesterday's clutter, she sat down and began staring into the mirror at the other end of the table. The face that looked back at her appeared almost unrecognizable. How long had she been playing other people? The years seemed a blur.

She took a moment to get her mind into Auntie Clara, and then began putting on the costume. First the middle-class dress, clean and well kept the way Clara liked it. It was a soft blue with simple embroidery. Her shoes were barely worn, as if Clara favored them and saved them for special occasions. Her wig was brown with a few tinges of gray. Using theatrical makeup, she went from a woman in her mid-twenties to a woman in her mid-sixties.

She donned a simple locket and grabbed a cane. Aunt Clara walked with a limp, the result of a disease that had crippled her left leg. Taking her purse, K began her journey.

With Aunt Clara's limp, moving quickly was not an option, which meant she proceeded toward the prison at an agonizingly slow pace. Ironically, creating the fake limp was causing her leg to knot up painfully, and thus the moment she got inside the prison, she needed to sit down.

"Can I help you, madam?" a stern voice called out, but as the speaker peered up at Aunt Clara, his face softened.

"Oh, good man, I know you are busy... I am Clara... Clara Blackmoor... I have come to visit my nephew. I've just arrived by boat from across the Halen Sea. I live far away and have only now been able to make the trip." Taking out a delicately embroidered handkerchief, she coughed into it. "I'm sorry..." She gave him a weak smile. "Been sick since a child, but I never let that bother me."

The guard's brow furrowed for a moment. From what he had read Merrin didn't have any relatives, but trying to verify that would take time, paperwork, effort. Scrutinizing the woman once more, he sighed, "Of course. Just give me a moment."

"Of course, dear." K sat and waited patiently. She had hoped the guards would be too lazy to verify family records, but no matter. She could always come up with more details to make her story believable. Coughing into her handkerchief, she glanced up when the large door opened and another young soldier appeared.

"This way, my lady." He gave a curt bow.

Getting up slowly, she headed over to the door as the soldier held out his arm for her. "Aren't you a sweet boy. I bet your parents are proud of you."

"They are, ma'am." He smiled down at her, supporting her arm and walking slowly with her.

"Thank you for allowing me to see my nephew." She patted his arm.

"Of course, but I warn you, my lady, he is in the darkest parts of the dungeon. It does not...smell well. Here..." He handed her a small satchel filled with cloves and orange peels.

"Thank you, my boy." Clara patted his arm. When the final dungeon door opened, K did her best not to recoil in disgust and tried to appear as dignified as possible while clutching the satchel to her nose. The young soldier brought her down to the bottom floor. There was barely any light except for a torch on the wall, which the soldier grabbed to light their way. The fetid stench of sweat, unwashed bodies, and festering filth was stifling.

"My, this is not what I expected," protested K. "What is in that room? I've heard of prisons having torture rooms. Is it true?" She pointed, shaking as if in fear.

The soldier squeezed her arm. "Do not worry. It is simply a storage room and access gates to our running water and sewage, thus the rather rancid odor down here. Keep that satchel to your nose, my lady."

He led her to a cell door and opened it. "Merrin, you have a visitor, your Aunt Clara," the soldier called as he lit the torches around the cells. Chains rattled and coughs echoed through the frigid chamber. Merrin's eyes lifted. He didn't have an Aunt Clara. He looked warily at the woman walking closer to him.

K bent down over her cane so she could get a closer look at his condition. "Oh, my poor boy, your Uncle Seph and I are so sorry for what happened and want you to know we are here for you, my boy, and to not lose hope. One day you will be free to sail the seas again." She sniffed the satchel, halfway tempted to shove it up her nostrils, so paralyzing was the dungeon's horrific smell.

By the gods, Merrin looked awful. He was thin, but it seemed he still had some muscle, which meant it wouldn't be too hard getting him out of here. *Dirty, unshaven, and smelling of the sewers—quite the catch!* She had to stop herself from giggling at her own private joke.

Merrin's lip flickered. "Thank you, Aunt Clara. I'm glad I have you to watch over me." His voice was hoarse. It seemed Sephtis was up to something, though what that might be he had no idea.

"Stay strong, my boy." She blew him kisses as the guard shut the door. "Does no one watch these prisoners?" She glanced around.

"Usually Lieutenant Henry does, but he's been having..." The young man seemed reluctant to say any more.

K patted his arm. "It's all right, dear."

"He's having issues with his marriage..." The guard leaned in toward K to whisper the rest into her ear: "His wife is having an affair and he keeps trying to catch her."

"Ohhh...now that's a shame. Poor man." With a sigh, she wrapped her arm around the young soldier's arm. "Such a sad thing to have family in prison..."

The soldier patted her hand and helped her back up the stairs when an older soldier appeared. "Lieutenant Sanders, what the hell do you think you are doing!!" he shouted, his face turning red.

The young man swallowed hard and frowned.

"Don't you dare yell at this good boy!" K exclaimed indignantly "He was doing the right thing and showing proper manners, which are clearly lost on you, sir!" She stamped her cane angrily.

The older soldier was a bit taken aback, not sure of what to make of this woman. "What were you doing?"

"She was visiting a relative, sir." Lieutenant Sanders wanted to laugh but held back. He liked this woman.

The older one frowned but finally nodded. "Fine, go on. Escort her out of the building."

Once they had made it outside, K reached into her purse and pulled out a few gold coins. "I can only assume that was Henry. Now go buy yourself an ale or three. I think with that prick you will need it at the end of the day."

The young soldier burst out laughing. "Thank you, Aunt Clara."

She flashed him a smile and a wink. "Of course, my boy."

Walking slowly with a limp, K headed away from the prison, her mind whirring like a top as she tried to figure out her next move. She was going to need a soldier's uniform. If Finnegan appeared at her place again tonight she would ask him to get one for her.

It was late afternoon when she finally made it back home, only to find Finnegan passed out in the bed again. How he always managed to make it past her locks! He was a tricky bastard when he wanted to be.

Well, at least she didn't have to go looking for him. Taking off her costume, she headed to the fire pit and swept out the old ashes into a nearby bucket. She would need to empty that soon, but not tonight. Taking the last of her kindling, she started up her fire, slowly adding logs once it got going. Heading to the wooden tub, she pulled a plug from the wall and rainwater rushed into it, filling it up quickly.

"I brought food," K heard Finnegan call out with a muffled voice.

"I want a bath first," K answered and watched as the stones grew hot from the flames. Grabbing the tongs, she picked them up and dropped them into the water one by one until it was nice and hot.

"I'll join you," Finnegan mumbled, having snuck up behind her.

"Aren't you digging up a body tonight?" she inquired as she glanced behind her to where he leaned sleepily against the wall.

"Not anymore. Sephtis found me and made me do it this morning, said it would be too late later." Finnegan shivered at the memory.

"Fine." K was too tired to argue. She began undressing, not caring about him seeing her naked. Their bond was forged in fire and neither crossed the line they each had drawn.

Finnegan dropped his clothes and stepped in first, making K roll her eyes. "A bit greedy today, aren't we?" she scoffed as she stepped into the bath opposite Finnegan and intertwined her legs with his. He grabbed the soap and began scrubbing his legs and hers. "I just want to get clean...at least for a little while," he insisted.

"All right." She smiled and leaned back, not minding his scrubbing. "When you're done, I'll get your back."

"That would be great," he sighed, scrubbing his chest and then handing her the soap. K grabbed it and quickly scrubbed herself up. She then motioned for him to turn around. He complied. Pouring water over his head from a pitcher, she scrubbed his back, then his hair. She used her nails to scratch lightly at his scalp. The pirate moaned happily.

Rinsing him off, she handed him the soap. "Your turn."

Nodding, he poured water down her thick, curly mahogany hair. He scrubbed it thoroughly, massaging her scalp and eliciting the same moan from her. "No wonder everyone thinks we are having sex," Finnegan chuckled.

K laughed. "I like them guessing."

"You like everyone guessing," Finnegan snorted.

"True." K shrugged.

Finnegan's fingers worked down her neck and collarbone. When his hand slipped over her right shoulder she flinched slightly. "Are you ever going to tell me about that?"

"Not yet. Someday...maybe."

After rinsing her clean, he stood, stepped out, headed to a cabinet and pulled out large sheets for them to dry themselves with. K got out, wrapped the sheet around her, and tied it, then headed to the small table and brushed out her hair.

"I brought some of your favorites." Finnegan pulled out some chocolates he knew she would like and was rewarded with a rare smile...a real smile.

"Where did you find them?" K rushed over eagerly.

Finnegan quickly pulled them away. "You will spoil your dinner."

"I don't care! I'm a big girl. I can make my own decisions." K was still trying to grab the package from Finnegan's hand, but he was just too tall for her to grasp it.

"Yes, well, I spent good coin on this dinner, so we are going to cook it and eat it...then you can have the chocolate." Finnegan was grinning again and her hazel eyes flashed.

"I could just climb you and get it, but I'm too tired," K said cheekily before she began unpacking the fresh bread, a package of beef and vegetables, and some fine spices. Heading to the table, she put a well-worn wood block down and began chopping the vegetables.

"You do have a skill in the kitchen. You know, you could always retire as a cook," Finnegan teased, settling down at the table and watching her every move.

"I don't think so. I do it because I have to, not because I like it." K spun the blade deftly in her hand before resuming her chopping. She ignored his intrusion as he repeatedly reached over to snag pieces of the bread and cheese she was cutting.

"Pity, you are good at it," he said as he snatched yet more morsels.

"I'm good at many things, or have you forgotten?" Her eyes lit up and she chuckled.

"Hahah, yes, there is only one thing I'm not sure you're good at." The corners of his eyes crinkled up.

"I assure you it is one of my best skills," K replied, pointing the knife at him.

"Is it *the* best skill?" Finnegan popped the cork on a bottle of wine and poured a couple of glasses.

"You will never know." K grabbed one of the glasses and took a long drink before putting some in the stew.

"Ha! Don't worry, one day I'll find one of your conquests and get all the dirty details." Finnegan poured her more wine.

"Good luck." K poured the rest of the ingredients into the pot and gave it a few stirs before looking up at him.

"Oh, you know I love a challenge." His eyes suddenly darkened.

K knew that look. He was thinking about Nora. "You will find her, Finnegan. Sephtis is back and he will scry some more for her."

Finnegan nodded. "I know." He seemed to be trying to convince himself.

"Speaking of the old bastard... Do I even want to know what he's doing with the body? I know the end plan, but this is...different."

"You know the usual magic potion, magical powers thing he does to prep the body. We are supposed to set out tomorrow for the island." Changing the subject, he added, "I put everything you need in your usual hiding spot."

"Okay, sounds good... You know, you are rather noble for a pirate." Her voice had a teasing lilt and the corners of her eyes crinkled for a moment before she returned to the pot, whose contents were starting to boil.

"Very funny," Finnegan growled and took another piece of bread. "Do you want some more wine?"

"Sure..." K took the wooden spoon and began stirring the stew. "Hey, do you think you can get me a soldier's uniform? I need it for my plan to get this Merrin out." She looked back at the noble pirate, who sat slouched on the old wooden chair. His well-chiseled chest and torso were still slightly damp from the bath and his sheet was wrapped precariously around his lap. Why did he always have to sit around her place half naked?

Finnegan ran his strong hands through his dark wavy hair. "Sure. Can it wait till tomorrow?"

K nodded. "Sure. It can wait."

"Good, good," Finnegan sighed, rose from the hard chair, and sat down in a plump, well-stuffed chair. "I love this chair." He leaned his head back.

Rolling her eyes, she remembered the first time he had seen the chair. Apparently Nora had one just like it in her house. Now he always retreated into it when he thought of her. "What was the last thing Sephtis was able to scry about Nora?"

"He said something about clouds, three mountains, and a forked river... He was going to find out where, but he got caught before we could find out more." He tucked his sheet around him some more as a sudden chill ran through him.

"There are mountains to the north..." K mused as she began ladling the stew into bowls. "But then there are a few to the east. Let's have him scry one more time..." K handed Finnegan one of the bowls, grabbed one for herself, and took a seat at the table. "Then we will go look."

Finnegan stood, walked to the table, and sat down with K. "You don't have to help me."

The grifter's brow rose. "How many times have you helped me? It's the least I can do. Besides... I'm a bit of a romantic." She murmured the last part.

"Really?" Smiling softly, he dug into the stew. "I doubt we'll ever have time..." The pirate frowned, leaning forward as he ate another spoonful. "Now that he has a new body for his experiment...we will be working nonstop getting him everything he needs. You know that? Remember last time? He ran us both to the verge of collapse."

"The price of obsession," K muttered. "And we all pay one way or another."

Chapter 4

When the morning sun could no longer be ignored, K got out of bed and found a soldier's full uniform lying across the table...as well as her chocolates. A quick smile lifted her lips as she picked up the package and opened it up. As she began popping the chocolates into her mouth, she wondered how he had been able to get the uniform so soon. She wasn't going to ask, though.

She quickly packed a bag with everything she might need. There was no coming back here after she headed into the prison—not for a long time, anyway. She wanted to make sure she left nothing of true importance behind.

Once her bag was packed and she was dressed, she locked everything up tight and headed toward the secret hiding place where Finnegan had left money for her. It was inside an abandoned building in a small floor chest under a few barrels. She would need to put it someplace safe, so she headed to the nearby woods where she had planned for her and Merrin to emerge from the prison's sewer tunnel. Searching around the heavy underbrush, she found an old hollowed-out log. Placing the chest inside the log, she undressed and then put her clothes into the log as well. Hurriedly, she donned the guard's uniform, cautiously glancing around her as she did so. Once she was dressed and sure everything was in place, she began heading toward the prison.

When she got there she went straight for the front door, closely watching the guards' movements, speech, and patterns as she advanced. With a nod, she headed into the fray. No one noticed her or thought her out of place. Once inside she headed behind the counters. Whoever was supposed to be manning the front was currently not there and she used the opportunity to swipe a set of keys, then glanced at the roster that listed who was watching the different cell levels. She noted the dungeon guard's name—Lieutenant Henry; what luck!—then proceeded to make her way down the stairs just as the front attendant appeared.

"Where are you headed, soldier?" a gravelly voice called to her. K paused and casually turned around.

"I'm relieving Lieutenant Henry early, sir. He's got an important family issue he needs to deal with, sir." As she said this, she was fervently hoping that Henry was indeed actually working today and that there hadn't been some sort of shift change. Breaking someone out on such short notice came with far too many hazards and she was going to give Sephtis an earful when she saw him again. She could feel herself starting to sweat; thankfully, so was everyone else around her.

"I never heard him mentioning that." The older soldier's brows drew together in consternation as he began looking through the roster.

Leaning in close, K explained in a whisper, "Well, he didn't really want it known...affairs and all that mess." This seemed to satisfy the soldier as he stopped looking through the roster and set it aside. K just hoped he wouldn't press her for a name.

The soldier's eyes grew in understanding. "Oh, all right, go on ahead."

"Thank you, sir." K nodded and continued to head downstairs. This was going better than she'd expected. She encountered other soldiers as she made her way down the next flight, but they simply nodded to her. Soon the final underground cells appeared. She placed her hand on the door, took in a breath, and readied herself.

Staring at the bloodstained wooden door, its rusty hinges about to give away to everyone that she was heading to the pit of despair, she did her best to prepare herself. K's slender hand wrapped around the handle and she grunted. Pulling down the lever and shoving it open, she made her way inside, trying not to gag.

A voice bellowed in the dull light, startling her. "What are you doing here, soldier? I've never seen you before!" Lieutenant Henry rose from his stool stationed by the dungeon door, one hand on his weapon. Noticing some food on a desk across from his station, K marveled that anyone could eat amid the stench wafting from the wretched hellhole just beyond the door. She strained to get a better look at Henry and was thankful for the low light as she did her best not to let her face give away her thoughts. He was of average build, but it looked like he drank too much and bathed too little.

K saluted. "I'm sorry, sir. I'm new. The name's McGregor, Private McGregor. General Lewis asked me to relieve you." She pointed up at the stairs. Thank goodness for the gossip of soldiers on her way in. "Said you were to head home immediately and not to stop for anything."

"Well, all right, private." The man stood up and handed her the keys. "Just ignore the prisoners, understood! No matter how much they pretend to be sick."

"Yes, sir!" she said, saluting.

Once the man had left and K could no longer hear the sound of his retreating footsteps, she locked the door behind her and rushed over to Merrin's cell, then began working through the keys trying to find one that would open it. "Come on, come on..." she mumbled in irritation. Finally the door creaked open. As she entered the cell, its rancid air hit her like a wall, and she felt vomit rising up into her throat. But she steeled herself and began working on Merrin's chains.

Merrin's eye slid open. "Didn't the beating already happen..." he groaned.

"This is your lucky day. You're getting out of here," K hissed with exertion, continuing to work at the shackles on Merrin's ankles until they finally came free. "Can you walk?"

Merrin stood unsteadily, grunting and grabbing at his sides. "Aunt Clara, I presume? Once you left, my weekly beating was due, again." He tried to get up, but faltered.

"Damn it." K wrapped her arm around him. "Let's hope I'm right about this," she muttered, dragging him to the next door. Behind this door was the supplies room, just as Sanders had said. She led Merrin inside. It was dark and cluttered, and she had to weave around stacks of supplies. She strained to listen for any sound that might help guide her way toward the escape route. Finally she heard running water. She moved as quickly as she could while dragging a wounded, moaning Merrin behind her. There on the ground lay a rusted grate layered in filth, the way to their freedom.

"Hold on just a minute." Setting him down, she used one of the keys to open the sewer grate. Then she opened the waterway's grate. Leaving the waterway grate unlocked, she grit her teeth.

"Come on, we need to get in." As she stared down the pitch-black abyss, a stench fouler than any she'd yet encountered emerged and brutalized her senses.

"Are you kidding me?" Merrin growled, looking down the hole. This was worse than anything he had ever imagined, though he knew it was the only way.

"Trust me, I'm not thrilled about this either!" K said through clenched teeth. "Come on." Sitting on the edge, she took a breath and held it as she lowered herself down first. She then turned around and helped Merrin down. Fortunately, the tunnel wasn't very tall, so she was able to lock the grate behind them by jumping up, grabbing onto its slats with her outstretched fingers, and pulling it into its locked position. Dropping back down, K kept her lips clenched tight until the splashing stopped, so as to prevent any of the putrid droplets from landing in her mouth. This was going to be horrible fun.

"All right, let's get the hell out of here." K wrapped her arm around Merrin and did her best to lift him up as they began walking through the sewers. Up above, soldiers were yelling "Where did...go?!...this way!" K was relieved that her ruse had worked. The soldiers didn't even give the sewers a second thought—no one would be that crazy.

"I think I'm going to be sick..." Merrin gagged and then, seconds later, pitched forward and threw up uncontrollably into the loathsome sludge coursing around his feet, some of which landed on K. "Sorry," he quickly said with a grunt of disgust.

"It's...fine," K sighed and swallowed the bile rising in her throat. The sound of rats skittering around made her eyes dart about. Rats—disease-ridden bastards.

It had been only a few years since the plague had been eradicated. Small rodents infused with the foul curse had been used in warfare against Chamberre and Ahris. The two nations bonded over the plague's eradication. Gareen feigned ignorance, but all knew that is where it originated and thus all neighboring nations had severed their ties with Gareen. They went so far as to erect a magical border through which only those with magical writs given by the King or Queen could pass. She had done her fair share of eradication; the creatures were wretched in their own way, covered in pustules. It was a mercy killing them all. K could hear fragments of frenzied conversation and footsteps clamoring above. "We think...water grate...sewer? It's death...sir."

At least with the dim light she could not see the rats, though she did listen carefully to ensure none came too near to her or Merrin. Just in case. Heaving Merrin up a bit higher, she trudged forward half carrying, half dragging the man through the tunnel, hoping that the grate with the door she had spied the previous night would soon appear. If she had only had more time to formulate a decent entrance and exit strategy, all this chaos could have been avoided.

"I don't know...how much...more I can...go," Merrin gasped, then gagged.

"Come on, just hold on a little more," K encouraged, gripping him a bit tighter and leaning more of his weight onto her. The weakness she had been prepared for—two years of doing nothing but sitting in a small cell can do that. But his beating had left him so drained he was barely able to move on his own, and the fact that they were wading through sewage was doing his wounds no favors.

"I'll try," Merrin forced through his gritted teeth. The thought of his children drove him as he forced one foot in front of the other. One step at a time through the vile slosh. There would be no saving them if he simply died here in this filth.

"You've got an iron will, don't you?" K smiled in the dark.

"So I've been told." *One foot after the other, Merrin.*

"Hey... I think I see the way out." K could see a stream of light and hear gulls crying. "Come on, we can do this. If I don't get you out, Sephtis will kill me." With a second wind she lifted Merrin and began moving quickly toward the grate.

"Sephtis... Why didn't he just have you break *him* out?" he grunted.

"I don't know, honestly. Sephtis has always had his reasons for what he does." Reaching the grate, she grasped for the wall and leaned Merrin against it once she found it. "If you have any strength left, don't sit down."

Reaching her slender arms through the bars, she ripped off the lock and pulled the weathered chains down. She shoved the rusted door open, turned around, and grabbed Merrin. "Come on, we are getting out of here." With a heavy grunt she pulled him through the door and shut it behind them, refastening the lock and doing her best to make it look undisturbed. After a few steps, the rancid air gave way to fresh clean sea air. The sound of soldiers was getting far too close. They must be readying search parties.

K continued pulling/dragging Merrin, and every so often she would shove both of them under the water when she got a strange feeling—a deep unease that would curl its way up her body and send a spark of urgency through her. Her sixth sense, created from years of deception and hiding in the shadows, made it so the soldiers' gazes never fell on them whenever they looked out from the battlements.

Merrin took in a deep breath and sighed. "Thank you."

"Don't thank me yet," said K, glancing around as they began walking through the now-salty water. "I still have to get you out of here." They were hidden by two grassy banks on either side, but the channel was getting smaller and smaller the closer they got to the beach. There was a straight line they could take through the trees, but it would leave them in plain view of the soldiers. Yet Merrin was in no condition for them to take any less straightforward a route.

"Look," pointed K. "There is a straight shot to the woods. Can you make it?" K looked around. She didn't see anyone, but that didn't mean there weren't eyes watching.

"There is a beached ship over there..." Merrin pointed. "Help me get there and I'll hide inside and wait for you to come back. I can make it that far."

K's brow rose. "Good idea." She gripped him tighter as they continued to sneak along the banks until the channel opened up to the beach. They then shuffled and stumbled their way to the old ship. K helped Merrin inside and then looked to make sure he wasn't visible to anyone.

"All right, are you good if I leave you for a while?" Her brow raised slightly as she looked him over.

"Go, I'll be fine." Merrin waved her ahead. "I'll just rest and gather my strength." Merrin closed his red, leaden eyes and began recovering his breath.

K stood and looked out toward the forest, then glanced back at Merrin. This was cutting it really close, but what choice did they have? She would make it work. Moving as fast as she could, she tore off the soldier's uniform, not caring that this would leave her in her small clothes. Burying the pieces in the sand, she sprinted into the woods toward the log that held her supplies. Money, clothes, and a knife—everything a girl needed. Scooping everything into her arms, she ran to a nearby stream, cleaned herself off, and put on her breeches, tunic, and leather corset.

Undisguised, she was the closest to herself she had allowed herself to be in some time. Tying her hair up tight, she put on her hat and attached her short blade to her hip. K hated wearing it—hated feeling it in her hand—but it was stupid to let herself or someone else go unprotected due to her aversion to the blade. Gathering the rest of her things, she made her way back to the ship where Merrin had fallen asleep. Moving slowly through the brush, she surveyed her surroundings and didn't sense anything amiss. If an ambush were going to happen, it would be now. Leaving the safety of the woods, she made her way into the empty bowels of the beached ship and crept toward where she had left Merrin.

"Hey, Merrin," she said, shaking him. There was no response. Panicked, she leaned farther over, shaking him again and whispering his name louder.

"What?" His voice was dry and hoarse. K sighed in relief. "I'm not dead, don't worry."

"Hmph, well, let's go. You need to clean up and I know just the place. It's nearby and they get paid to keep their mouths shut." K held her hand out and helped Merrin to his feet.

K supported Merrin as they both stepped out of the hideaway. Relief washed over them as they saw that night had fallen. The cover of darkness would make it easier to escape notice, and the short respite Merrin had enjoyed seemed to have done him some good, as evidenced by the fact that he barely needed K's help walking.

"Where are we going?" he asked, blinking. Even though it was dark, the light from the stars and moon was still painful to eyes that had grown accustomed to the darkness of the dungeon. He rubbed his eyes, trying to make the ache go away.

K glanced back. "Don't worry. We will get you some healing potions that will help fix that right up. Luckily we are right next to the underbelly of our lovely city. Soldiers rarely visit, and when they do, this is the last place they will go. We are going to an inn that caters to us lowlifes." K chuckled as they made their way into the city.

Merrin stiffened. "I am not a lowlife."

"Easy boy, just a joke. But as of right now you're an escaped convict, a murderer—no matter how noble your intentions were or how innocent you are. You know this." Her voice turned whimsical. "It will make you that much more of a dashing character."

"What do you mean?" he asked, looking over at her as they weaved through the underbrush and trees and finally emerged onto cobblestone. Merrin looked around surprised. He had never been to this part of the city. He hadn't realized how close it was to the forest.

"Nothing... Here we are." She pulled him down an alley and to the back of the inn. There before them was an old blue door with a small window. K rapped on the glass. When it began to open, she shoved in a bag of coins. After a pause, the door opened all the way up. She had given exactly one gold, two silvers, and four coppers. If the combination had been wrong, she would have been skewered.

"Hello, K," a deep voice echoed from inside a stone hall lit with torches illuminating a very clean and well-decorated space. Luxuriant paintings and tapestries adorned the walls. Candelabras could be seen running down the halls. The stone ground had red carpeting festooned with gold and black designs. The innkeeper had once been a notorious thief, and so vast were his spoils that he managed to run quite the thriving black market out of his little hideaway. He had a penchant for the finer things in life and for anything he viewed as unique and beautiful. K was an enigma to him and he adored her for it.

Striding over to where he stood, K said, "Hey, Tops, I need a room." She didn't even bother with introductions. "One that is hidden, preferably."

"Of course, only the best for you." The towering man with a smooth, deep voice bowed and smiled at her. "This way..." He motioned for her to follow him. K glanced over at Merrin, making sure he was still able to hold his own before she briskly followed. "I am pleased you chose my establishment first."

With a fond smirk, K quipped, "I wouldn't go anywhere else to lay my nefarious head... Well, unless I'm working." She winked at him, making the large man laugh.

"You are the best grifter I know, K," he said, opening up the door for her. Inside was a large four-poster bed with gilded engravings, lush feather pillows and blankets, and a thick soft mattress. Finely carved furniture decorated the room, showing off Top's exquisite taste. "Is there anything you need?"

"Yes, a hot bath in my room, and then can you come back later? Let me get settled and I will have a list and coin for you." K smiled up at him.

"Of course." Tops nodded. "I'll have the men bring a tub and hot water for you." K reflected that for such a large man he knew how to disappear quickly.

"Well, Merrin, let's get you inside." K turned to help him, but he had already gone inside and was sitting in a chair rubbing the red velvet.

"I bet you were thinking I'd lead you to some hovel." She chuckled and set her bag down. She turned to shut the door but was stopped by several men and women who appeared with a large tub. They proceeded to bring the tub inside, set it down, and fill it with hot water. Then, as quickly as they had stormed in, they left. "You can never say Tops isn't on top of things."

"I hope that's for me." Merrin looked longingly at the water.

"It most certainly is," she said, taking the bottles she had requested and pouring their contents into the steaming water. One was for healing, one was for soothing, and one was for cleansing.

Merrin took off his clothes and K politely turned around while he finished undressing and stepped into the tub, hissing as the water stung his wounds. Grabbing the soap and sponge, he began methodically scrubbing while K started figuring out what they would need to get out of the city. Before she could get him the new wardrobe, she needed to see what he would become first.

"Merrin, what did you do before you went to prison?" K turned her head slightly back so that she could read his face as he answered.

"I worked on the docks checking shipments in for the O'Conners," he answered, scrubbing up his hair.

"Anything before that?"

"I was the captain of the ship for my father-in-law... Well, he wasn't my father-in-law yet and technically he disowned Penelope when she married me..." His voice trailed.

"Ahhh, that...that we can work with," K said as her mind whirred around what new person Merrin was about to become.

"What are you talking about?" Merrin asked curiously as he concertedly rubbed the soap onto his skin, determined to wash away the years of filth and the recent sewer expedition.

K stood and walked over to him, pulling a chair next to the tub. "I will give it to you plainly, Merrin. You can't be Merrin Blackmoor anymore... He needs to be dead, forgotten, for now at least. You need to create a new identity and I will help you. Now, have you always had a beard?"

"No, I was once clean-shaven. Is this really necessary?" he asked before dunking down to rinse his hair. When he came back up, some of the grime had begun to wash away, revealing what appeared to be flaxen strands of hair. Even with the beard he was a striking man, despite this current gaunt appearance.

"Oh, yes, if you wish to live." She smirked at him. "That blonde hair will need to go... We are going to change you into the opposite of what you were. Pirate Captain Killian Voltaire. The men will wish to *be you* and the women to *be with you* when I'm done." Hazel eyes lit up with excitement. "Or some sort of combination, whichever you fancy."

Merrin realized he had no choice; he had to embrace this new life. "Killian, aye? I had a cousin named Killian after my great-grandfather. Not a bad name...but Voltaire?"

"Would you prefer something else?" K folded her arms and raised her brow at him.

"I just don't know where it's from." Suddenly realizing how stupid he sounded, he avoided her gaze for a moment.

"It's foreign, but don't worry, it's from your mother's side. You chose it because your father was an asshole who left you and your mother destitute. You took to the seas at a young age as a cabin boy to the renowned pirate Red Beard, who took you under his wing, and now you are the captain of your own ship," K rattled off to him as she paced the room.

Merrin paused in the middle of his scrubbing. "Did you just come up with all that right now?" he asked incredulously.

K shrugged. "It's a gift."

"Indeed, it is. So, I heard the man call you K; is that short for something?" he asked, trying to be as polite as he could be at the moment.

"It's what people call me." K tilted her head at Merrin, her gaze scrutinizing him.

"Hmmm, an aunt, a soldier, a grifter...a chameleon, then."

K couldn't help but laugh. "If you stay in there any longer you will turn into a prune. I don't need you wasting away any more than you already have." Getting up from her chair, she headed to her list, scribbled down several more things, filled up a bag with gold, and gave the bag a shake.

As if on cue, there was a knock. "It's Tops, K."

K opened the door and laughed. "I bet you heard those gold coins clinking all the way upstairs."

"I have excellent hearing when it comes to coin." He flashed her a wide wicked smile.

K handed Tops a scroll and the bag of coins. "Will you get these things for me, please?"

"Of course, and I brought food for you and your...friend," he chuckled. The girl with the serving tray rushed in and placed everything on the table, then left. Tops looked over the list and nodded. "Don't worry, I'll be back in a few hours with what you need."

"Thank you, Tops." K smiled and shut the door behind her. Merrin was at the table with a sheet wrapped completely around him. Was the future Pirate Captain Voltaire a bit of a prude?

"Don't eat too much or you'll puke. I promise you'll have good food for days to come." Sitting down, she took his plate, mashed the potatoes, and added a bit of milk and butter. She then added chunks of chicken, took away the greasy duck, and put down a few vegetables. "Here, eat this first...then we will see how you feel."

Merrin growled at her but decided to listen. She had been right so far. Eating this meal brought him such joy and agony all at the same time. His small stomach grumbled angrily and he had to stop eating.

"Here, drink some wine." She poured him a glass, noting the mix of euphoria and pain that flashed across his face.

"So, how do you know Sephtis?" Merrin asked, taking a sip of the deep red wine and smiling.

K shrugged. "I work for him doing various jobs. Right now my job is to get you to his private island."

Wine shot out of Merrin's mouth. "His private island?" he exclaimed.

K's brow rose. "I take it he didn't tell you. Well, yes, he has a private island. I will let him explain the rest." K downed the glass of wine and poured another, not willing to say any more. Who knows what Sephtis told him and she didn't want to ruin anything.

Merrin sighed. "All right...I guess this really is happening." He took a long steady drink of wine before setting the empty glass now. "So what now?"

"Now we begin creating Killian Voltaire."

"Let's just use Voltaire," Merrin murmured.

For the next few hours they discussed Voltaire's history, how he became the pirate that he was. K made Merrin repeat the name over and over, along with the names of family members, until she was satisfied he had committed them to memory. When he finally got tired of saying his name, there was a knock on the door.

"Right on time." K smiled and opened the door. "Thanks, Tops. I appreciate it."

"You're welcome, K. Stay as long as you need."

Returning to the table she began removing the bag's contents, which included a shaving kit, boots, clothes, and jewelry.

"Let's get your hair cut and your beard shaved, shall we?" Taking him to the chair, she began slicing off his hair, cutting it close to his head. Then she skillfully worked his wild, matted mane of a beard down to an immaculate short boxed beard. Taking a gold hoop earring, she sighed, "This is going to sting."

"Wha...OWW!" he shouted, pulling away from her and touching his throbbing, slightly bloody ear.

"Sorry, but I have to say...it works on you." She cocked her head appraisingly as she looked him over. Even underweight, he was handsome. "Sorry. Here, drink these potions—they'll help you. Sephtis sent them and they should put you back on your feet. But I think you've been through enough today."

Merrin lay on the bed. "My name is Voltaire..." he murmured. "Voltaire." Once he was asleep, K sat down on the chaise lounge and closed her eyes with exhaustion.

Both slept until late and it was K who woke up first. Stretching, she got up from the chair and slipped out to get breakfast. When she returned Merrin was sitting up in the bed rubbing his face.

"Did you sleep well?" K asked as she set out the food.

"I did. It was the best sleep I've had in a long time." He gave her a smile for the first time.

"Good! Now I have your clothes here for you." The pieces were laid out separately.

"That's a lot of black." He shook his head smiling.

"Well...you are a pirate..." she reminded him slowly and shrugged. "Now, leather breeches, black tunic with high collar and silver embroidered, leather vest with silver buckles and black leather coat three-quarter length, and leather boots."

He took the clothes and began putting them on piece by piece, feeling as if he were becoming more and more Voltaire with each additional piece. Once he was done he turned to K. "What now?"

K's eyes glittered. "Now put these rings on your thumb and forefinger, then this silver ruby ring on your pointer finger."

"Really?" he chuckled. "Are you sure we have enough jewelry?"

"You are right..." Digging in the bag, she found a silver pendant. Perfect. "Here." She walked over to him and clasped it around his neck, letting the pendant fall to his chest. "Now you look like a pirate."

"Are you serious...with this much jewelry?" He did not believe it for one second.

"Pirates love their gold, their silver, and their jewels and gems. Trust me. Now just a few more things..." Looking through her makeup, she pulled out some black eyeliner. She pushed Voltaire down onto the seat, lined his eyes with just a little of the eyeliner, and then smudged it. It all looked great except that damn bright blonde hair.

"There is one more thing." She had almost completely forgotten about it. The blonde hair had to go and she knew just the thing to get rid of it, having purchased several throughout her life. Taking out a small dark vial, she held it out to him and said, "Drink this and it will dye your hair black. Don't worry, later on you can get something to turn it back to blonde or whatever color you prefer."

"I can't believe I'm doing all this..." Taking the bottle, he drank it down and in seconds his silken flaxen hairs turned obsidian. "Well, how do I look?"

K was staring at him. Gods, he looked amazing. "You are now Killian Voltaire." Beaming, she grabbed his hand and brought him to a mirror. "I do good work."

Merrin didn't even recognize himself. As he leaned in to the mirror to take a look at his new self, he ran his fingers over his beard and saw Killian Voltaire—pirate captain, renegade, swashbuckler, ladies' man. "You're right." He turned to look at her. "I am Killian Voltaire."

"Well, then, Captain Voltaire, let's go find you a ship," K said with a triumphant nod.

Voltaire's eyes lit up. "Oh, now, *that* I like—but I get to pick her out and her crew."

"As you wish. Come on, handsome." Winking, K spun around and headed toward the door.

Voltaire watched her hesitantly for a moment. Was he ready to do this? Taking a deep breath, he committed himself and then followed quickly behind. As they walked, his mind settled and he began to think of his wife and kids...His kids. "K, I have to find my kids!" He rushed up to her and put his hand on her arm in a panic.

K involuntarily flinched. "Don't worry. Sephtis is taking care of that."

Voltaire didn't even notice her reaction. "Really?" he said, the relief evident in his voice.

"Really. Now let's go. We are close to the shipyard." K waved at Voltaire to follow her as she weaved through the back alleys. She grit her teeth as her pace quickened. She hated the way she always flinched when someone touched her shoulder. She was thankful Voltaire was too frantic about his children to notice it. Finnegan was the only one who could do it without her jerking away and it had taken a while for her to get to the point with him.

The closer they got, the more excited Voltaire became. He was enlivened by the smell of the salt air and the sound of the waves and men working on the large ships. As he moved past K, his eyes avidly scanned the line of ships. They were beautiful. The golden sun was high, making it a perfect day to sail. His blood pumped faster in his veins. The ache to be out on the sea was building within him.

The harbormaster was a stout heavy man with only a ring of hair around his head. If he had been wearing a robe someone might have mistaken him for a monk...or a friar.

"Harbormaster!" Voltaire called and flashed a charming smile as he sauntered over to him.

The man looked up. "What can I do for you?" There was no inflection in his tone, not even a hint of inquiry, really.

"Do you have a ship for sale? Preferably a galleon...I know that's a tall order. Perhaps there is another harbor?" Voltaire paused, waiting for the man to say something, anything.

The harbormaster shuffled over to the large book and began paging through it. "There is a ship...the *Wicked Damsel.* It's not really for sale, but the captain's in serious debt. He might be willing to sell...if you have the coin."

Voltaire sighed. It was a hard thing separating a captain from his ship. He would know.

"It's the last one on the dock. Good luck," The harbormaster snorted.

Voltaire turned around to K. "What do you think? We got the coin?"

K had been watching Voltaire and was impressed. He had taken to his new role so naturally. And Finnegan had been right: he was handsome.

"K..." Voltaire called again.

Her lips curled. Yes, Finnegan would hate it if she told him that she thought so...Oh, now she couldn't wait to see him. This was going to be fun.

"K!" he shouted at her.

"What? Oh..." she laughed "Yeah, don't worry."

Voltaire's brows drew together for a moment as he wondered what she was thinking. What had made her light up like that? "Well, let's go, then. We have a ship to try and buy."

"Lead the way, Captain Voltaire." K held her hand out and bowed slightly.

With a curt nod and a swagger, he made his way down the docks toward the large ship. Men were sitting around on the empty boxes. A large tap keg sat atop one box and the men filled their mugs from it as they worked on repairing nets. They were grumbling at each other. All eyes were on Voltaire as he headed toward them.

"Who are you?" a slightly drunken voice called out as Voltaire came down the plank.

"My name is Killian Voltaire and I have come here with an offer of a new life, a new chance, perhaps even a new adventure." The pirate smiled and placed his hands on his hips.

"Really, how do you propose that?" The aged captain tossed the bottle into the water.

Voltaire motioned to K, who stepped forward and, setting her bag down, pulled out a decent-sized chest. Seeing the way K handled the chest made Voltaire reflect that she was definitely stronger than she looked. "This is enough gold to get you out of debt with your men and whoever else you may be indebted to." He popped the chest open and allowed the pirate to look inside.

The pirate's men jumped up. Seeing the gold, they all began talking amongst themselves at once.

"So what do I have to do for this chest of gold?" The captain rubbed his beard and glanced at his men.

Voltaire looked up at the ship. "Your vessel, the *Wicked Damsel.*"

"Auch...you ask a lot of a man," he growled looking at his ship with possessiveness. Then, hearing the grumble of his men, he backed down. "Let's go..." he sighed resignedly. He motioned for them to follow him.

Voltaire and K followed the older sailor up the plank and into his private cabin. "She needs a little bit of work but not too much," the old man said, rooting around a chest and finally pulling out the title of the ship. "Her title...take care of her, boy, and she will take care of you."

"Don't worry, she will be in good hands." Voltaire nodded at K and she handed the old man the chest. With a curt bow the pirate turned and walked away, leaving Voltaire and K alone aboard the ship. Below them they could hear the men cheering in elation at their unexpected bounty.

With the transaction completed, the two took a minute to look around the room. It had at one time been opulent, but was now run down. The velvet seats were torn and the sheets were a dungy brown. The floor was sticky with unknown substances.

"So what do you think?" K said, sitting down on a plush chair. If the cabin's condition were any indication, this whole vessel was likely in need of cleaning and repair.

"I'm not sure yet. Let me go take a look around first, then I'll be back and let you know." Voltaire smiled slightly, feeling the first stirrings of excitement beginning to build.

"I'll be here." K smiled wearily.

Chapter 5

Sephtis and Finnegan were already en route to the island. Finnegan was standing guard in front of the door leading into a room in the bay of the ship. The old mage had asked not to be disturbed. The rituals he performed took time and he could not abide any interruptions.

Sitting on a rickety old chair with his feet stretched out, he twirled a knife in his dexterous fingers. She was fine. K was fine. There was no need to worry. But worry still gnawed at him, and in a pique of frustration he lashed out savagely, throwing his blade into the beam with a bone-jarring thunk. He stood, walked up to the beam, and took the blade out for the hundredth time.

"You keep that up, you will wear through that beam and we will all be in trouble," Sephtis's voice sounded behind him.

"Are you done?" Finnegan asked, sounding harsher than usual.

"I am... Come here." He motioned for the pirate to follow him.

Finnegan frowned, not really sure he wanted to see whatever it was Sephtis had hidden down there, but he went along. As soon as he set foot into the room, he froze. There, encased in a crystal-looking coffin, lay the body of Penelope Blackmoor. Taking a few steps toward it, he looked down. She looked nothing like the dead body he had pulled out of the ground. Her hair and body were clean. Her skin was flush as if she were still alive. Was it...possible?

"Is she—" He turned to the mage in surprise and a bit of shock.

"No, I was able to bring her body back to the state it was in before death, but she is nothing but an empty shell right now..." His voice held awe. This was how far he had gotten last time, but something had gone wrong in the ritual. He didn't have the right tools and the body had burned. He had tried to get a new body but was caught and ended up in jail. But now he had another chance.

"What about Nora?" Finnegan finally brought up his lost love, feeling he had been patient enough.

"Ahhh, I've been wondering when you were going to ask. Thought you may have forgotten, with how close you and K are," Sephtis chuckled.

"K and I are friends," Finnegan retorted, ignoring the smirk on Sephtis's face.

"Right..." Sephtis's voice turned placating. "Well, once we reach the island and get Penelope in the lab, I will get everything ready for another scrying. By then hopefully K will be back with Merrin." A mysterious smile pulled on the old man's lips. Though he didn't look so old now... In fact, he looked younger. The blessings of strong magic.

"I am holding you to it, old man." There was a slight warning in his voice as he spoke these words, but as the gravity of the situation dawned on him, his face took on the shadow of deep concern. "Come on, you've been in there for days. You need to eat." As much as this mage drove him crazy, he cared for him.

Sephtis nodded. "Yes, I am a bit hungry."

"Come on, I'm sure Craig is cooking up something somewhat...edible." Finnegan said, opening the door.

"We shall see." Sephtis sighed and headed toward the galley.

Chapter 6

Voltaire sat on the bench at the dive inn, his bright eyes watching the men and women around him as he sipped his wine. The ship inspection had gone well. The old man had been right: there were a few things that needed fixing and cleaning, but all in all she was sturdy. The smell of pine, tar mixed with rope, and various other smells was like coming home to him.

"So, see anybody you would like to hire?" K asked, ignoring the stares and comments as she sat down and kicked her feet up on the old table. No one here would care about the transgression. This inn was so shady even *she* felt a bit unnerved being there. Ever vigilant against would-be thieves, she kept her hands close to her coin purse and dagger.

"A few." he said appraisingly. "I'll speak to them later, when they're sober." He smirked. It was best to see the men at their worst first. Sailors always drank to relieve boredom and tension on the sea, but some behaved very stupidly and belligerently when drunk. When Voltaire saw this behavior in men who were drinking, he knew which ones *not* to ask to come aboard his ship. The last thing he needed was a hothead who would put his own life and those of the ship's other crew members at risk.

"All right, I'm heading back to Tops. I'm tired. Are you coming?" K stood up, having had enough of the seedy tavern and the lecherous gazes of the men inside.

"I'll be right behind you." He smiled, watching her sashay away. Once she was out of sight he frowned and set his glass down, putting his head in his hands. Penelope... She was gone. What was he going to do? She was gone... His kids! Gods, not chasing after them was killing him. Part of him thought about just taking off now and looking for them, but he owed Sephtis for getting him out of jail and keeping him alive during his captivity. With a sigh he got up, left a few coins on the table, pulled the collar up on his jacket, and headed outside. As he turned into the alley, he heard the familiar sounds of a struggle and went toward it.

"Get off me, you pig!" a female voice shrieked in the darkness. This was followed by a sharp smack and an angry grunt.

"Get off my sister!" another voice yelled, and Voltaire heard bones breaking. He arrived just as the aggressor fell onto the ground writhing in pain. Standing over him was a heavily muscled lad and a pretty young woman.

"What's going on here?" Captain Voltaire inquired. His voice was nonchalant but his eyes were watchful. His hand rested casually on his blade.

"These street rats attacked me!" the ill-dressed man said as he struggled to get up. He was in clothes much too small for him. Obviously he had robbed some noble, taken the man's clothes, and forced himself into them. *Not a bright one.* The captain's eyes scanned the man.

"That's not true!" the young woman yelled, her eyes darting about as the strong arms of her brother held her in a tight embrace, one hand stroking her hair.

"I tend to side with the street rats..." Captain flashed an apologetic smile. "His words, not mine. I suggest you run along while you still have your sack, man."

The guy growled angrily but realized he was no match at this point and took off.

"Well, that was an ugly bit of business." Voltaire turned to his two new acquaintances. "Who are you and how old are you?" Best to get all the information up front, then he could decide what to do with these two urchins... Well, not really urchins; they were adults, albeit young adults.

"My name is Leon and this is my sister Fleuette. We are the same age—twenty." The tall man ran his fingers through his reddish hair, pulling it away from his face.

"How long have you been on the streets?" Captain inquired. Leon was definitely well built. He was average in height with good muscle tone; it was obvious he worked hard. But he still looked overly lean, his face somewhat gaunt.

Large shoulders shrugged. "Since we can remember. Our parents died when we were young. We've been running the streets ever since, doing odd jobs to stay alive. We were working on a galleon to gain passage here...hoped to find a better opportunity."

"So you two know your way around a ship, then." Voltaire started to smile. This might have been a most fortuitous run-in.

"Aye, we do. I can man the sails and handle the wheel. Fleuette can read the maps, knows how to fix up wounds, and she cooks better than anyone I've ever met. We know how to repair and clean." The large man smiled affectionately down at his sister.

"Well, then, you're hired. I need crew members aboard my ship... It's the *Wicked Damsel.* You can start by cleaning the cabins. The old captain was a bit...lax with his cleanliness." He tossed them a small bag of coins. "To start with."

"Really!? Oh, thank you, monsieur!" Leon shook Voltaire's hand firmly.

The captain chuckled and smiled. "Now, now, no need to get too sentimental. Head on over. You are the first, so don't worry about meeting anyone else there." Voltaire nodded to them and made his way toward Tops Inn.

Not needing to go the back way, he walked through the front door and into the main tavern. Eyes immediately turned to him. A young wench sauntered seductively up to him with her hips swaying and her fulsome breasts straining against a too-tight corset. Her dress shone pink and orange like a vibrant summer sunset. Her hair was hitched up high with feathers. The makeup around her eyes made them piercingly blue—as if they were made to bore into men's innermost carnal desires—and bold red lipstick accentuated her sultry lips.

"Would you like some company tonight?" she purred, her arms wrapped around him.

"You are a lovely lass, but no." He smiled sadly, the pain of Penelope too fresh in his mind. Not that it wasn't tempting.

The girl pouted at him until a look from K sent her scurrying.

"Ah, my rescuer and my protector. K, I thought you were sleeping." He turned to see the grifter walking over to him, glass in hand. He could tell from the reverent stares of the men and women around that they regarded K with tremendous respect. A few even looked at her in awe.

"Oh, of course not. I just prefer something a bit more refined than the swill of the Sow's Teat...which, by the way, is a horrible name for an inn!" K shook her head laughing.

"Yes, yes, it is. Well, you will be pleased to know I have a map reader, a cook, and a sailor already hired. Tomorrow I will find the rest of the men and hire them." He gave K a cocky smile.

K nodded. "Excellent. I got you your own room." She tossed him a set of keys. "It's across from mine. I figured you might like a night alone before you have to sleep with a crew of men snoring, drinking, and singing."

"Not such a bad thing when you have the captain's quarters," he chuckled.

"Rub it in, Voltaire, rub it in," she snorted and headed back down the stairs.

Chapter 7

Voltaire and K stood at the docks looking up at the ship. The men he hired were off gathering supplies and saying goodbyes to family.

"Do you know where we are going?" he asked. Glancing over at K, he noticed she seemed a bit tense and anxious.

"I do. One of the men is getting us a map. The old captain's was so worn I could barely read it." Her eyes glanced around, never settling, as her mind kept returning to the thought of soldiers catching up to them and tossing them into the dungeon—or worse.

"We will set sail as soon as everyone is aboard. Come on." He motioned with his head and the two headed up the plank.

"Captain Voltaire!" Leon rushed over to him. "Welcome back aboard, Captain! Fleuette and I have been trying to ready the ship for you!"

"Good lad! K, this is Leon. Leon, this is K, my lovely savior."

Leon's gray eyes widened. "It's an honor, my lady."

K's eyes lit up. *Oh he's adorable,* she thought. "The pleasure is mine. You have done such a wonderful job for such a short period of time." K gave him a quick nod before turning to walk toward the doorway that led to the cabins.

"My sister and I work hard." He paused, looking toward the door and glimpsing the top of Fluette's head through the small window. "Oh, and there she is." Leon opened the door before Fluette could. Standing in the doorway now was a young woman with chin-length sandy brown hair that glowed red in the early morning sunlight. Storm-gray eyes widened and her pale lips parted, letting out a sound of surprise.

"Fluette, this is K, Captain's first mate." Leon assumed this was her rank, given how highly Voltaire spoke of her.

"Oh, it's a pleasure." She curtsied slightly.

"Fluette...lovely name! A bit long. Do you have a middle name?" Voltaire asked, smiling.

"Lilly, Captain," Fluette replied slightly breathless, her cheeks flushing pink.

"Lilly it is," Voltaire said with a firm nod.

K shook her head. "Well, Lilly, how about you show me to my cabin? I'm dying to finally set this down," she said under the pain of the bag's heavy strain on her back.

"Of course, this way." The young girl motioned K to follow her.

K followed along, wondering about the young woman in front of her. What was her story? There was so much more going on behind those stormy eyes and unassuming presence. Whatever it was, she would make a great character for a disguise, the grifter mused.

Lilly opened the door to the room next to the captain's quarters. "Wow! You did an amazing job! I looked at these rooms the other night and they were pretty bad." She walked over to the bed. "Did you wash the linens? Was there even soap on board?" Her voice filled with mirth.

Lilly laughed feeling nervous around this worldly and beautiful woman. "Yes, actually, a lot. It seems they bought a lot with the intention of cleaning and never did." The petite girl kept her hands clasped together, her eyes watchful.

"Well, I am glad because I was planning on sleeping on the chair until the linen was clean. Now I actually get a bed. Thank you." K bowed her head slightly in appreciation at the girl. In a way she reminded K of herself.

"Y-y-you're welcome," Lilly stuttered. "I better go. So much more to do."

"Sure." K nodded, setting her bag down on the round table.

Moments later there was a knock at the door. "Come in!" K said, thinking it was Lilly again.

Voltaire strode in and quickly spun around to avert his eyes from K, who was walking around in her small clothes. "Do you have a habit of running around half naked?" he asked, calmly staring at the wall.

"Well, to be honest, I thought it was Lilly, but yes. It *is* my room. I should be able to walk around completely naked if I want to." She smirked, putting on her clothes.

"It *is* your right as First Mate," Captain noted.

"True..." she chuckled. Finnegan would have found a way to make this situation much more sexual than it needed to be...bugger... Hopefully he was miserable eating Craig's food and getting no sleep playing manservant to Sephtis! She snorted. It's not how she really felt. Not that she would admit it. "All right, you can turn around."

Voltaire spun around, visibly relieved she was back in clothing. "Do you know anything about sailing?"

"Why, yes, I do... I know a lot of things. Some of which I wish I could forget," she sighed indignantly.

"Good. Can you come with me? We need to set course." His voice easily slipped into that of a man in charge.

"Lead the way, Captain." K's eyes glittered with newfound respect as she marveled at how well he fit into his new role. *I wonder if we'll actually do some raiding... I would love to see my new creation in action.*

The Captain's room looked so different now that everything was cleaned and organized. On the massive table lay the map. "Well, then, let's see." Walking over to the desk, she took a quick look and pointed to a spot on the map. "Right here...this is the island we need to head to."

"Leon and Lilly won't be pleased to learn they are heading back where they came from." Chamberre bordered Ahris and the two countries had always been on civil terms. Trade had always been good. Chamberre had several small islands at its northern point that were well known for their fruits and wine.

"So tell me, how did you meet the twins?" she asked, sitting down and grabbing the bottle of wine.

"On my way back to Tops some bastard was trying to have his way with Lilly but wasn't expecting her brother to be there. Just some poor kids trying to make a living and barely scraping by." His voice held a bit of bitterness.

"You speak as if you're ancient and not just a few years older..." she snorted. "And you gave them an opportunity. You are a good guy, aren't you?" Using a knife, she popped out the cork. Taking two glasses, she poured wine in both and handed one to him.

"I am... I was... I don't know what I'm supposed to be now," he said as he sat down, sighed, took the glass from K, and then stared out at the island." And I feel ancient," he groused.

"I know it's hard right now, but I promise it will get better. It has to." Her lip flickered in commiseration and she took a drink of wine.

The two sat in silence for a few moments, both thinking of their own pasts and troubles that had led them to where they were now. The silence was broken by a knock on the door.

"Captain, we are ready to set sail."

"Thank you, Leon," Voltaire called and stood up. "The first mate and I will be out in a moment. Shall we?" He bowed slightly to K.

"Yes... Let this adventure begin."

Chapter 8

The *Wicked Damsel* eagerly set sail, her black sails filling with wind. It seemed as though the weather was even in their favor. The first few nights went by peacefully. Lilly proved to be not only a miracle worker at organizing and cleaning but a rather good chef as well. Voltaire had handed her a few maps of their course and asked her to keep an eye on things, to which she gladly agreed. The men for the most part left her alone, though there were a few who let their eyes linger too long on her. Leon put an end to this whenever he saw it by growling loudly, which sent the men scurrying away hastily.

Lilly had begun to feel safe in her new station. On the captain's orders, she had been sharing a cabin with her brother for the sake of ensuring her safety and comfort. Most of the men assumed K was sleeping with Voltaire, something K found amusing. And Lilly...was jealous. Since the moment she'd first seen the dashing captain in the alley she had been smitten. But it seemed she was invisible to him.

Several nights had passed uneventfully. The crew definitely appreciated Lilly's cooking, often complimenting her while they ate. One particular night after dinner she was standing in front of the large barrel washing dishes. A slurred voice called out to her. "Oy, luv, you do make a fine beef stew." Unsure who the drunken compliment came from, Lilly turned around. Seeing Jonas a few feet behind her, she immediately tensed. When they had met he'd been affable enough, but she knew all too well how a few drinks could change a man.

"Umm, thank you." She grabbed another dish and put it back in the water, her hand fishing around for a knife. He was getting closer; she could feel the heat of his body behind her. She found the knife and gripped its handle tightly.

"You are a pretty little thing..." he slurred, wrapping his arm around her shoulders clumsily. She quickly brought up the knife, but it slipped out of her wet hands and back into the barrel. Her heart began to race, but relief washed over her a moment later when she heard Voltaire's voice echoing in the galley.

"Now, that is no way to treat a lovely lass, Jonas," he chided angrily, his eyes dark and glowering. He knew even as he said this, though, that nothing truly awful had happened yet, and that Jonas was not the kind to hurt a lady. He was just an idiot and a drunk.

"Captain... I... Sorry, lass," Jonas sputtered as he quickly let her go.

"Get out of here, Jonas," the captain hissed and gestured for the hapless drunk to leave. "And if you ever go near her again, I will gut you myself." His eyes were slits. He hoped he had scared the ever-loving shit out of the other man and that word of this encounter would travel.

"Yes, sir!" He took off, leaving the captain and Lilly alone in the room.

Voltaire watched him leave, then looked back at Lilly, his eyes softening as he did so. She was pale but holding her composure. "Are you all right? Jonas is a drunken fool and I'll make sure he gets punished in the morning..." Not wanting to give her another scare, he was careful not to move at all.

"I am— Captain— Thank you. I didn't sense any real danger from him. He just...scared me." Her stormy gray eyes flickered like lightning as she looked up at him.

Voltaire's brows drew together for a moment as he regarded her. Such an innocent soul. Pretty, delicate, just like her namesake. "Good. Let me walk you back to your cabin."

"Oh, all right," she said, and then, glancing back, added, "There are dishes still."

"Leave them, it will be fine." As they approached the door to the hallway, he smiled and stepped back, letting her through the door first. She moved in front of him and headed toward her cabin, feeling butterflies in her stomach. His footsteps echoed behind her. Reaching her door, she turned around and smiled. "Thank you again, Captain...for everything." Before he could respond she disappeared into the room and Voltaire could hear Leon's voice.

Heading up to the bridge he dismissed the man at the wheel. He wanted time to think. His sleep was now full of restlessness. All he could see was his beloved. There was no chance to say goodbye...no chance to make peace. In trying to save her he had condemned her.
"Forgive me, Penelope... I failed you," he mourned to himself, revealing briefly his broken soul.

K stood at the staircase just below the bridge, her figure hidden by the overhang, and frowned upon hearing the sadness in Voltaire's voice.

"Did he... Did he lose someone?" A soft voice spoke behind K and she turned to see Lilly. "His wife," she replied. "She died recently."

"Oh... No wonder he looks so sad when he thinks no one is watching."

K's lip flickered—the little flower had a crush on the captain. It was sweet, actually. "What are you doing out here, Lilly?"

"Leon found out about Jonas... He's *talking* to him." Lilly quickly told K what had happened.

"Will it get physical?" Not that she was worried. A fight would be rather interesting. Before Lilly could answer there was an eruption of shouts and a loud thud below deck. "I guess there is my answer."

"Go get the captain." K flashed a quick smile and then took off down the stairs.

Sighing in annoyance, Lilly ran up the stairs to the bridge. "Captain Voltaire," she said as she rounded the top of the stairs and made her way to the captain. "I'm sorry, Leon knew something was wrong and I told him about what happened... I can't hide things from him. He's gone after him."

Voltaire smiled. "Well, I can't fault him for that. Come." He motioned with his hand for her to follow him.

Lilly nodded and trailed behind him down to where Leon had just knocked Jonas out cold.

"Leon, good for you." Captain Voltaire passed him by and made his way over to where the rest of the men stood whispering amongst themselves as they gawked at the aftermath. Kneeling down he checked the man over. It was just a good crack to the nose. Lots of blood and he would feel it for a while, but no permanent damage done.

"Let this be a lesson to all of you. Haggis, take him back to his room. The rest of you...as you were."

He came to Leon, pulled him aside, and in a conciliatory tone said, "I understand your need to protect your sister, but I *dealt with it.* You going over my head undermines my authority." His voice softening, he quietly added, "That said, nice punch." He grinned and clapped Leon on the shoulder.

"I'm sorry, Captain... I've been the only one to look out for her..." His head dropped and his brow furrowed in remorse.

"I know, and don't worry about it. It will be all right." Voltaire patted the man's shoulder again. "Besides, I would have done the same thing in your position."

"Thanks, Captain." Glancing down at his knuckles he noticed for the first time how badly they were bleeding.

Lilly came to him and took him by one of his bloodied hands. "Come on, let me fix you up." She smiled.

"Don't tell me you're a *healer,* too," K teased, bemused at Lilly's show of tenderness toward her brother.

"Yes, she is," Leon boasted. " No real magical training, but a lot of natural talent."

Lilly quickly turned several shades of red. "Come on, Leon." She hastily pulled him down the hall toward the stairs.

"Why are you embarrassed?" Leon asked as she pulled him into their cabin.

"No, it's just— I'm not a very good mage. All I can do is heal simple things." Lilly sighed, placed her hand over his, and closed her eyes in concentration.

"Well, you did bring all those dead vegetables back to life so we didn't starve." Leon looked down at her.

She met his gaze "Oh yes, now that is the true power of a mage—turning a bunch of dying plants edible." Snorting, she checked his hand over and dropped it, then put her hands on her hips. "I can look after myself, Leon. You don't always have to come to my rescue."

"What are big brothers for?" Leon shrugged, smiling at her, and then his brow furrowed. "I meant what I said, though, Fluetta..." he said, using her first name to show his sincerity. "I may have protected us. But you *saved* us."

Chapter 9

Finnegan solemnly walked with Sephtis up the overgrown, winding path to the palace. Penelope's body lay in a crystal coffin behind them, carried by several men on either side. The light was fading and everyone knew that darkness emboldened the local predators. The men quickened their pace, not wanting to be caught out in the dark.

"I will be glad to get home," Sephtis sighed as they struggled up the hill. Glancing back, he saw one of the men stumble, making them all scramble to readjust the coffin, their brows covered in sweat and panic in their eyes. "Be careful with her!" he snapped. Abashed, the men scrambled to steady the coffin.

Finnegan would just be happy to sleep in a decent bed. He longed for the soft, comfortable bed he had slept in with K (though he ignored the thoughts of K sleeping next to him).

After cutting through a thicket of brambles and underbrush, they reached an overgrown wrought iron gate. Cutting down several of the vines, he turned to Sephtis, who held out a large key. Taking it, he shoved it into the lock—praying the old thing wouldn't break—until he heard the familiar click and eagerly began pushing it open. Cutting a path through the old walkway, he made his way inside, quickly followed by Sephtis.

At the sight of the vast, opulent mansion that was Sephtis's home, the wearied men shook off their fatigue and began sprinting toward the entrance. They unlocked the door and stepped inside. "You." Sephtis pointed to the men holding Penelope. "Follow me," he said as he disappeared deep into the mansion while Finnegan found his old room, which was right next to K's. He opened the window to let in the air and went around the room dusting the furnishings. He knew K would be home soon, so he opened the window to her room to let it air out as well.

Once his room was settled he fell into bed and passed out.

Meanwhile Sephtis set up the coffin on the large table against the back wall of his workshop. Pulling out the old tome of magical spells, he looked for his scrying spell. As much as he wanted to keep on with his research, he had promised Finnegan that he would scry for his lost love.

Rubbing his brow he put his hands on his hips and looked around the room. "Where did I put that blasted map?" The map had cost a pretty penny. It had all three realms, their cities, and their topography, both land and sea. He noticed a pot in the corner with a large scroll sticking out of it. "Aha!" Sephtis carefully unrolled the map onto the large table, using various crystals to hold the curled edges down and help amplify his power. This was going to take a lot out of him and he was grateful for the rest he had been able to get aboard the ship. He pulled the crystal pendulum up over his head and held onto the golden chain in his left hand while using a small crystal-embedded knife to cut his wrist just enough to let the blood drip down into his hand and coat the crystal. In the same breath he dropped the crystal and began chanting as the pendulum began to sway steadily around.

Sephtis's eyes clouded over as the magic took control. He remembered in his last vision there had been clouds, three mountains, and a river. He focused on that image as he willed the crystal, through words and thoughts, to show him where Nora was. This would have been so much easier if he had had something of hers to work from, but lacking that he was forced to do a cold scry, an arduous affair. Still, he pressed on and with each scrying attempt came closer to the vision he sought.

While Finnegan slept and Sephtis scryed, the sailors and servants set to cleaning the main house and the servants' housing. It had been a little over a year since they had all been in the mansion. Sephtis may have been a hard man to work for, but he always ensured the people who worked for him were paid fairly and had decent lodgings. He was often generous, even when cantankerous, which made many of them very loyal. Getting everything in order would be a bit of a task, but it wouldn't take them too long.

The next morning, Finnegan made his way down the stairs into the kitchen, where the servants were busy making breakfast. "Has anyone seen Sephtis?" he asked, grabbing an apple. The servants shook their heads and he tossed the apple into the air, caught it, and took a bite from it. "Probably downstairs," he concluded with a shrug.

Leaving the servants to their work, Finnegan walked through the side hallways to the stairs leading to the laboratory. As he went down the stairs, he heard chanting coming from inside the room and realized it was Sephtis. He stopped himself and frowned. If it was Nora he was scrying for, Finnegan didn't want to screw it up by interrupting. He decided instead to head outside and check on the other men. He was glad to find that they were staying out of trouble for the most part.

The scene was one of joyous exuberance. The men played games and sang, clearly enjoying their time on land. Finnegan let it go for now. It wouldn't be long before they would be back at sea heading to god knows where for god knows what, just for Sephtis's sake.

The sun slowly began to set and Sephtis still had not emerged from his room. Finnegan sat on the chair just a ways outside the door. As the last orange tendrils disappeared, he saw Sephtis's door slowly open. Finnegan looked over at the old man, who looked deathly pale. He knew Sephtis would be hungry and tired. He rose, went to the kitchen, and grabbed some bread, cheese, and butter. He slathered the butter on the bread, then added the slices of cheese. As he turned to set food on the table, Sephtis came and sat down with a heavy grunt. Without a word or much sign of enthusiasm, Sephtis began eating.

"You look like shit, Sephtis," said Finnegan. "What have you been doing?" he asked as he pulled out a mug, filled it up with mead, and set it down in front of the mage. "Here, drink this and head to bed."

Straining to speak, his voice dry and scratchy, Sephtis answered, "I got a bit closer to where your Nora is. She is in Chamberre to the far north. I will need to scry again to get a bit closer to her location. It would take months, if not years, to search with what I have right now." Seeing the sudden flash in Finnegan's eyes, Sephtis promised, "I will find where she is and soon you will be free to go find her. But I still have work to do and I need your help, understood?"

Finnegan's fists clenched. "Understood."

The god of the seas had continued his blessing on the *Wicked Damsel* with a rather decent journey. As the island began to appear, K found herself feeling a mixture of excitement and worry. Seeing Finnegan again and showing him her new creation would be great fun, but who knew what tasks Sephtis would have planned for them. Nothing easy—*that* she was sure of. She had let on a little bit to Voltaire about Sephtis, details that she knew the mage wouldn't mind her sharing.

Looking out with her spyglass, she saw the island's shore and that the *Layla Rising* (named after Sephtis's wife) was already docked. K put the spyglass away and was watching as they pulled up. "There are cabins near the main house that the men can stay in," she informed Voltaire.

"I don't want to leave Lilly with all those men," he objected, hands on his hips. "Even with Leon watching her, it's just not wise." His bright blue eyes were watching everything but came to rest on Lilly, who was trying to adjust her pack on her back but having trouble.

K's lip gave a knowing flicker. "Sure, she and Leon can join us," she simpered.

The *Wicked Damsel* closed the remaining distance to the island and the crew docked her on the shore. Men from the *Layla* came aboard and greeted K as she made her way down the plank. Voltaire motioned for Leon and Lilly to come with him, and the two followed eagerly, wide-eyed and excited for their new adventure. When their feet hit the white sandy beach they marveled at the pristineness of it all. For a moment they wondered if this mage had conjured someone to come clean his beach for him. Up ahead were the beginnings of a trail that led into what looked like a jungle of trees, bushes, vines, and strange animal sounds. The mansion sat upon a hill overlooking the island. Its white marble and rust-red roofing sat high above all the green foliage. A smaller building surrounding the mansion had the same white stone walls and rust tile roofs.

K spotted the path that had already been cut out for them by Finnegan. "Come on, I'm sure Sephtis is eagerly awaiting your appearance." K motioned for the group to follow her. "Watch your step. It can be a bit tricky getting there."

As they approached the final stretch everyone was glad to be done with the hike. It had proven every bit as tricky as K had said it would be, even with the path cleared. Once they were in view of the door, it swung wide open and Sephtis walked out. "Well done, K! Faster than I had expected!" Sephtis gave her an approving nod. K glanced behind Sephtis to see Finnegan emerge and join him at the front steps.

"Merrin, it's so good to see you!" Sephtis was smiling brightly at seeing his friend looking so well.

K put her arm over Voltaire's shoulder. "It's me, remember? And *his* name is Killian Voltaire, dashing pirate captain of the *Wicked Damsel* now." K grinned widely.

Finnegan's eyes narrowed and he frowned, immediately disliking Merrin, Killian, Voltaire—whatever his name was. Ignoring Voltaire, he looked back at the other two behind them. "Who are they?" He asked in a gruffer than usual sound.

Voltaire looked over at Finnegan, who was just a bit taller and more heavily built. "This is Lilly and Leon. They are with me. Is there a problem, chap?" He tilted his head.

"I'm not your chap and..." Before he could finish, Sephtis cut in.

"It's fine. Come, Mer— I mean, Voltaire. I have much to discuss with you. Finnegan, find the two young ones rooms." He waved his hand at Voltaire who smiled and followed his friend.

"It is so good to see you," beamed Sephtis "I promised I would take care of you and I will."

"K mentioned you were going to look for my kids?" Voltaire asked eagerly. Then, turning back to K, he gave her a wave and a smile. "I'll talk to you later, K." before returning to follow Sephtis.

"Finnegan found the orphanage, but they had sold the children and we found the name of the ship they were sent on, which had already set sail. I promise we will go find them, but there is something I wish to discuss with you." he brought him to a small study where the walls were lined with bookshelves, and a heavy desk in the center was heaped with scrolls. Motioning for him to sit on the leather chair, he sat on the one across from it.

"What do you wish to talk about?" Voltaire asked, watching as Sephtis—who looked so different in the light of day—was pouring each of them a glass of whiskey.

Sephtis handed Voltaire one of the glasses and sat down. "What if I told you there was a way for you to be with your wife again? And no, I don't mean you dying."

Voltaire froze...the chance to be with Penelope again...not just that...he doubted she would ever want to be with him again, but to give her another chance—the pain, the guilt was so overwhelming. "I would do whatever it took."

"I am glad you said that, my friend, because I have a way of bringing her back. I lack only the proper tools. If you, K, and Finnegan can get them for me, I can do it." His voice resonated with passion and urgency.

"I don't understand. She's buried..." Voltaire shook his head.

"Come, I need to show you something." Voltaire got up and followed Sephtis to the back of the mansion and down the stairs. Sephtis paused at the door. "I need you to prepare yourself."

Opening the door, he walked in, followed by Voltaire, who froze.

The room was a larger version of his study. The walls had floor-to-ceiling bookshelves filled with books, but unlike in his study, here crystals, potions, and strange artifacts also adorned the shelves. Runes covered the ground, walls, and ceiling, but what held the captain's attention was at the room's far end, encased in crystal.

"Penelope..." he whispered and started walking, then paused, unsure of what his reaction would be. Taking a breath, he steadied himself, headed to the back wall, then walked up the stairs to the coffin. "She looks like she's sleeping..." He reached out and touched the coffin, stroking it right above where her cheek was. "I failed you..." His voice broke and his fists clenched. His iron will broke and he rested his head on the crystal coffin, tears rolling down his cheeks. "I love you, Penelope. And I will get you back even if you hate me. You can at least have a life." His voice was hoarse as he made the vow.

Sephtis knew all too well how Voltaire felt. It was a pain he was all too familiar with. "I will give you some time. When you are ready, come back to the study. I will be there waiting for you," the old mage said quietly and disappeared.

Meanwhile Finnegan had led the twins to their own rooms and they were eagerly enjoying the luxurious accommodations. K followed and leaned against the banister, and once Finnegan had re-emerged from the last room, she tilted her head.

"How was your trip? Did you enjoy Craig's food?" K was just starting her teasing.

"It was fine... I see you are rather cozy with the new and *dashing Captain Voltaire of the Wicked Damsel*," he snorted, his eyes flashing.

She was about to joke about how she thought Voltaire was a bit more handsome than Finnegan, but held back. Finnegan was on edge and upset. "There is nothing between Voltaire and me, Finn..." She rarely used his nickname, always feeling it a bit too intimate. "He's still in love with his wife and it's not me who has a crush on him...that would be the little flower who watches him with doe eyes." She was standing in front of him, her head tilted up to look at him. "Are you mad at me?"

Finnegan looked down at her and his eyes softened. "No, K, I'm not. I'm just frustrated. Sephtis did another scrying session and he got closer to where Nora is...up north in Chamberre, by the mountains, three rivers..." He tossed his hands up in the air. "I am so close to her...and stuck waiting. You know I hate waiting." He ran his hands through his hair and interlaced his fingers.

"I know you do. How about we go get something to eat for right now, hmm? And don't worry. We will find her and you and she will live happily ever after." She was smiling at him but found it forced, and for some reason her stomach dropped.

Finnegan nodded. "You are right, K, as usual." Sighing, he dropped his hands to his side. "Come on, Minx, let's get that belly of yours fed. You know how cranky you get when you don't eat." He smiled broadly at her.

"You are right as well," she chuckled. "What sounds good?"

The two walked down the stairs side by side. Eventually Finnegan gently put his arm around K's shoulder, and though she flinched a little, she didn't move away.

"We probably won't see the both of them for a while. You want to play cards after we eat?" Finnegan asked as they walked into the kitchen. Servants were bustling about cleaning and filling the cupboards with food from the garden and animals hunted on the island.

"Sure, sounds good." K smiled. "Maybe we could invite the twins if they haven't died from euphoria."

Finnegan laughed. "Yeah, they seemed a bit excited."

The twins ran down the stairs toward the kitchen and slowed down before they ran into Finnegan and K. Lilly's eyes widened at seeing Finnegan's arm around K.

"Hey, you two." K glanced back at them. "Are you guys hungry?"

"Yeah, actually," Leon said, stretching.

The servants quickly began making something to eat and setting the table in the kitchen.

"You two want to play cards after dinner with K and me?" Finnegan asked the two who were sitting down at the table looking slightly wide-eyed.

"Sure, I used to play cards all the time to earn a little extra money," Leon said, relaxing and leaning back.

"Great, then you won't mind losing a few hands to me," Finnegan said, cocky as ever and pulling K's chair out. "I'll go get us some good wine from the cellar."

When he was gone, K leaned back in her chair.

"Are you and Finnegan..." Lilly finally got the courage to ask.

"Hmm? No, we are just friends." K flashed a slight smile. Looking at the two innocent siblings, she realized she needed to tell them the truth about what they were doing, give them a chance to back out. "I think it best to inform the both of you that Voltaire's real name is Merrin Blackmoor. I broke him out of jail, where he was serving a sentence for killing a noble man who was attacking his wife. His wife recently died and Sephtis is a necromancer working to bring her back. Staying with us means danger in a variety of forms. If you are not comfortable with this, no harm done. We will bring you to wherever you wish to go when we leave. Take your time to think on it if you need to." Her face was cold and serious.

"No need to think about it," Leon replied quickly. "We are in."

K nodded. "So be it." Glancing over, she saw Finnegan with a few bottles "You brought the blackberry, didn't you?" It was her favorite.

"Of course I did. You have such a sweet tooth, I'm surprised it hasn't leaked into your nature," Finnegan teased.

Her eyes narrowed. "Like your noble spirit leaked into yours?" she rejoined teasingly.

"You walk a fine line with me, minx." He set the bottle in front of her.

"Which do you prefer, red or white?" he asked the twins.

"Anything would be amazing," Leon answered and Lilly nodded.

Finnegan popped both bottles and poured several glasses. "Well, we will just drink it all."

Lilly giggled and took a glass of white.

A few hours later they were all drinking and laughing, slightly inebriated. The three bottles he brought up turned to six, then eight as they had dinner. Cards were a bit of a fiasco because none of them could focus long enough to even play their game.

Sephtis and Voltaire finally emerged from the laboratory, stopping in the doorway and shaking their heads. "You four need to head to bed," Sephtis growled.

"Oh, Sephtis, so cranky, old man." Finnegan stood and for a moment felt like he was back on the deck of the *Layla*, his body weaving with the rolling waves. "Come, K, boss wants us in bed."

"Fine, fine." She got up and then sat back down. Finnegan laughed, grabbed her waist, tossed her over his shoulder, and began carrying her toward the stairs.

Leon stood, picked up Lilly—who had already fallen asleep—and began carrying her toward the stairs as well. "Good night, Captain... Sir." He seemed a bit less drunk than the rest.

"What a mess," Sephtis growled in irritation. He hated messes.

"Let it go. They are blowing off steam." Voltaire gave a tired and worn smile. Servants quickly cleared the table and began putting new plates down.

"Let's eat. I need my strength. I have scrying I need to do in the next few days, then I will have the first tool we need." Sephtis motioned.

"The sooner, the better. I need to get my kids back." Voltaire sat down.

"And you will," the old mage promised.

Chapter 10

Finnegan carried K up the stairs, slung over his shoulder.

"Oh...don't move so much! You are going to make me throw up," K grumbled and then saw Leon pushing the door open to put Lilly to bed.

"I'm doing what I can. If you'd stop wiggling I'd be able to walk steadier," Finnegan growled. Reaching the door to his room, he struggled to grasp its handle. It was being unruly, constantly moving around. Finally grabbing hold of it, he managed to open the door and stumble into the room. Fumbling over to the bed, he pulled K off his shoulder, gently placed her on the mattress, pushed her over to the far side, and crawled in beside her. He knew he wouldn't be able to make it to his own bed.

"I need to get these clothes off..." K pouted, struggling to remove her corset. "Come on!" she growled.

"Hold on." Finnegan crawled closer, his fingers trying to undo the laces when he finally just ripped the corset, pulled it off her, and threw it to the ground. "Better?" He looked down at her, a hand on each side of her as she squirmed beneath him. His brow rose and he heard boots hitting the ground, then a moment later her breeches shimmied off.

"There! Now I can sleep," she sighed and curled up in a fetal position, falling instantly asleep.

"Happy to help," he murmured, falling down next to her. His last thought as he drifted off was that her hair smelled like berries. Unbeknownst to him, in the middle of the night his body wound up wrapped around hers, his face buried in her hair.

When morning came, K groaned as the sun's bright rays demanded her to wake. With a soft grumble, she rolled around and found her face planted into Finnegan's chest. It was startling at first. He smelled like pine, cedar, and something else she couldn't put her finger on. Whatever it was, it smelled great, and if she had been more conscious she would have pulled away—but, still in a haze, she rubbed her face against his chest until she felt comfortable and began drifting off to sleep again.

The two slept for several more hours until they both finally began to wake. Finnegan was on his back, his arms around the slowly waking K. The grifter lifted her head and pulled herself up, her long hair falling around his chest and tickling it. Chuckling, he brushed her hair back and tucked it behind her ears. She looked down at him for a moment and then smiled genuinely. "Are you hungry?"

"Starving," he said, returning her grin. "Let's eat."

Leaning back, she sat down on his thighs for a moment. "You tore apart my corset last night! It was expensive!" She shook her head, laughing as she stared at the tattered pieces on the ground. For a moment she wished she had been a bit more sober to witness that.

"I will buy you a new one." Finnegan sat up and placed his hands gently on her hips. "And don't tell me you have nothing to wear, my lady. You have more clothes than the Queen herself," he teased, pushing her off him gently so he could get up and stretch. They both were staunchly ignoring the sudden pull of desire between them.

"Oh, I do. I have many things to wear...each belonging to a character! I suppose I could steal from one of them." She walked over to the closet, pulled it open, looked around inside, and finally took out a heavily brocaded corset with an off-the-shoulder shirt. It was moss green and gold.

Finnegan waited until she was done dressing and smiled. "I like that color on you."

"You do?" She looked down at herself as she braided her long hair to the side.

"Yes, it makes your hazel eyes look a bit more green." He got up and headed to the door. K ignored the slight flush of her cheeks and she punched Finnegan on the shoulder.

"What is that for?" He rubbed his arm.

"For my corset. Now you don't have to buy me a new one. You can save your money for your gift for Nora." She forced a smile.

For a moment he thought she seemed almost sad...but he brushed it off. "Thanks! I will need to get something great for her, though I have no idea what."

Finnegan and K reached the top of the stairs, where Leon was waiting for Lilly.

"Morning, Leon." K watched him quizzically for a moment. She was still trying to figure him out. He had a good heart, that was for sure, but other than that he still seemed a bit of a mystery.

"Morning." He nodded, smiling slightly as he saw K watching him.

"Lilly okay?" Finnegan asked, not seeing the little mage.

"She is. She's just getting dressed." Leon motioned toward her door. "She's a bit overwhelmed by what she saw in the closet." A small smile lifted his lips.

A few moments later the once-raggedy-looking Lilly was now beautifully dressed in a blue dress with silver embroidery. Her hair was adorned with flowers and ribbon. Finnegan's brow rose with surprise at seeing her in a dress.

"Don't you look lovely!" K said, smiling. It was one the dresses from a character she had made and retired, on account of her having been killed violently in the course of one of K's ruses. "Help yourself to anything in that closet."

"I hope it's all right. My other dress was so dirty..." Her voice trailed.

"It's fine. Come on, let's go meet the old man and the captain." K took the lead as she always did, and Finnegan, hands in his pockets, whistled and followed her.

Chapter 11

For the next few days, Sephtis locked himself in his laboratory. He was scrying not only for Nora's final location but also that of the first tool he would need to summon Penelope's soul from the beyond.

The crew was making repairs to the ships and getting them both stocked for their next voyages. Though they were only taking one ship, Sephtis always liked having the other one ready just in case. Meanwhile K, Voltaire, and the others told tales and learned a bit more of one another's pasts. Voltaire learned of Nora, Finnegan learned of Leon and Lilly's upbringing, but no one learned anything new about K. She would not divulge anything, and when others pressed for information, Finnegan shut them down rather quickly.

They were sitting in the massive library by the fireplace and drinking wine when Sephtis finally emerged. Finnegan scrambled up. "Did you find her?!"

The old mage leaned against the wall and nodded. "I did. She is in the north of Chamberre in a small town called Gafton, and luck must be on our side because the Twisted Forest lies just to the northeast. In that forest is a tree over five thousand years old... I need amber stones from the sap of that tree." He ran his fingers shakily through his hair.

Finnegan's brow furrowed. He was about to get up, but Voltaire beat him to it. "Come on, old friend, let's get you something to eat and off to bed. We will take care of the rest." Captain helped the mage back toward the kitchen.

K stood up. "All right, time for bed. We need to be up early. Sephtis will want us to leave at first light. Finnegan..." she didn't even have to finish because he was instantly up and ready to go.

"I got it, K. I'll let the crew know. We will be running a nice full crew on the *Wicked Damsel.* Should be an easy trip." Finnegan was thrilled. Gafton... His beloved was in Gafton. With light steps he left the mansion and headed to the main cabin where they all gathered to drink and began spreading the news.

K sat in the library alone for a moment when Voltaire rejoined her. "You not heading to bed?" he asked, sitting down next to her.

Staring into the fire, K started to speak. "Voltaire..." her brow furrowed. "You do know what you're doing with Sephtis is dangerous? It is a forbidden magic for a reason." She tore her gaze from the flames to look at him.

Voltaire paused and leaned forward, clasping his hands. "If there is a chance to see my Penelope again, to be with her and the kids, to have my family back...it is worth it...whatever the cost," he growled angrily, but then he realized she was trying to be a friend. "But I appreciate your concern."

"Just remember something for me, Voltaire..." She stood up, hesitantly put her hand on his shoulder, and leaned down so only he could hear. "Sephtis is a good man, but he is single-minded when it comes to his desire to bring his family back."

Chapter 12

Voltaire stood at the bridge watching as everyone began boarding and heading off to work. It would be a short trip to Chamberre. Sephtis had given him the name of the ship that had taken his children. Sephtis's hours of scrying had again produced something fruitful. With the name in hand, he would begin asking around at the port to see if the ship had docked there.

Finnegan was great at getting the men ready and shouting orders. For her part, K was routing their path toward the city of Gafton and then the Twisted Forest. Soon the massive galleon pulled away from the island and began its journey to Chamberre.

Leon had already been a bit nervous because of all the additional men on the ship. He was on even higher alert now, but a nod from Voltaire calmed him.

A few days later they were already off and on their way.

The five of them sat in the captain's quarters looking at the map.

"So it's going to take two to three weeks to get to Gafton, depending on how the weather is. There are a few towns along the way we can stop at to get supplies, so we don't have to load up the moment we dock." K motioned. "But once we reach the border here to the Twisted Forest, we need to stock up from the nearest town. Who knows how long it will take us to find this tree."

Lilly leaned forward. "I used to hear tales of the Twisted Forest. Men going in and never coming back. It was rumored to have been where the first necromancer made himself known. Francois Twist. Driven by the desire to live forever, he used up all the magic within the forest to keep himself alive. The once living and beautiful forest was drained of all life and color and even now, thousands of years later, the forest is barely coming back to life." Her delicate fingers ran along the line of the forest's boundary on the map.

K shifted slightly. "Either way, we will need to ask around. Maybe someone knows about the tree. Sephtis told me it's the crying tree or tree of tears..." Smiling, she saw Lilly light up. "Have another story for us, Lilly?"

Blushing slightly, she nodded. "The crying tree was said to be the physical embodiment of the spirit of the forest and she weeps for her dead children. Through the years those tears hardened, turning to amber. The amber carried within it the magic of her spirit."

Voltaire chuckled. "Are you sure you're not a bard as well, Lilly?" he said with admiration. "With how you tell your tales you should be! You have us all enraptured."

Her eyes widened and her cheeks turned red. "Oh...n-no I, I don't sing well...at all."

"I find that hard to believe." Voltaire smiled.

"It's true," she sighed. "Just ask Leon."

All eyes turned to Leon. "My sister has many talents; singing is not one of them." He smiled wryly.

"Finnegan, I assume we will be losing you in Gafton." Voltaire gave a small smile. "Probably for several months locked in a room."

Finnegan chuckled and leaned back. "Sorry, but yes."

K turned her head, bent over, and began digging into her bag. Her chest tightened and she felt sick to her stomach. *Finnegan no longer there...leaving...perhaps never coming back. He was her friend...her best friend.*

"Find something interesting down there?" Finnegan asked.

"I did, actually. Not that I'll share it with you," she teased, having regained her composure and sitting up.

"Mmmhmm, you will one day." He winked. "When we dock, K and I will gather supplies. Leon, if you and Lilly could help Voltaire in looking for the *Mermaid's Quest*? That was the ship that his children were on."

"Of course, anything to help." Lilly nodded.

"We will ask around about that tree as well, see what we can find," Leon added.

"Excellent. We have a plan, then. Now let's go eat, drink, and be merry!" Voltaire's hands slammed the table as he stood up.

Chapter 13

Once the *Wicked Damsel* made port, Voltaire paid his men well and they eagerly headed into town. It was a crisp fall morning and the trees had already changed. Their leaves had turned from bright green to yellow, red, and orange and were littering the streets, making the ground just as colorful as the treetops had been just a little while before. In the distance storm clouds loomed, but for the moment the sky was clear, bright, and beautiful. He, Leon, and Lilly made their way to the harbormaster. Asking about the *Mermaid's Quest,* they found it had docked here for supplies and then left for the old country. No cargo or people were taken off the ship, meaning Voltaire's children were still on it.

It took all of his willpower not to jump back on his ship and head toward the old country, but he had made Sephtis a promise and he owed him. Sensing Voltaire's frustration, Lilly reassuringly put her hand on his arm.

"It will be all right, Voltaire," she said, her voice soft as she looked up at him. "You will find them." Leon shook his head when he saw her hand on Voltaire's arm and headed into a nearby inn to ask about the tree.

Voltaire looked down at her and smiled sadly. "Thank you, luv. Now, shall we go find that brother of yours and see if K and Finnegan have gotten what we need?"

Lilly nodded and reluctantly began to let Voltaire go when he took her hands, put them back on his arm, and patted them gently. He was thinking of keeping her safe from the men and she was doing her best not to fall even harder for the dashing Captain Voltaire.

Voltaire and Lilly walked into the inn. It was clean and simple. A few merchants were talking business at one table and a few middle-class patrons had gathered on their lunch breaks to eat and drink. They found Leon sitting at a table with a pint of ale.

"Find nothing?" Voltaire asked, sounding slightly defeated.

Leon shook his head. "They've heard of the forest but not the tree."

Eyes were following both Voltaire and Lilly. He pulled out a chair for her and she sat down. Sitting next to her, he waved his hand at the barmaid, motioning for two more ales. Moments later they were joined by Finnegan and K.

"Drinks already? We are a bad influence." Finnegan chuckled and sat down, followed by K. "Did you find anything out?"

Voltaire nodded, his lips pulling down to a frown. "It looks as though they went to the old country."

K rubbed her brow, feeling a sudden throbbing. "After we get the amber we can swing by before we return to Sephtis. It's a fairly lawless place, but we have enough coin to get the information we need."

"Sephtis said I needed to ret—"

"Sephtis will be fine," K snapped. "As long as he gets his amber, it will be fine. Trust me, I've worked with him longer than all of you."

Finnegan nodded, noting K's tone. "I agree with K." He glanced over at her. She had been tense and irritable the last few days. He wasn't quite sure what to say or do. Deep down he knew what was troubling her, but what could he do? He ran his hand over his brow for a moment, then rubbed his face to get rid of the nagging voice in his head.

"Weather is supposed to get pretty bad in the next few days, storms and such—so be prepared to get soaked," Lilly added, desperately trying to change the subject in an attempt to lighten the mood. Everyone had suddenly become anxious or angry and she hated the feeling.

"I guess that means we will need to get tents." Finnegan got up. "Come on, let's get the tents and get moving."

Leon finished his drink and stood up. "Are the men going to be okay?"

"They will be fine. I gave them each enough gold to keep them busy," Voltaire said, following Leon.

The group headed to the nearest general store and bought two large tents that Leon and Finnegan carried while Voltaire went ahead and carried Lilly's. Once they were sure they had all their supplies, they began making their way on foot. There were not a lot of horses for sale at the docks, though they were told that farther north, in the city of Dupon, there was a large livery that held horses.

Once they got there they would purchase horses to try to cut down their travel time, something Finnegan was more than willing to pay extra for. In silence the group walked along the dirt road, everyone lost in thought.

The road was lined with grasslands, and whichever way one turned one could see farmland, and every once in a while a cluster of trees. There was no natural shelter in which to take refuge should the heavens decide to open up and weep. Finnegan fingered the box in his pocket. It held a ring which he planned to give to Nora...He had proposed to her before she was taken from him and they were to be married. He wondered if she still had the original ring he had proposed with. Probably not—they would have sold it off first thing after they kidnapped her. Hearing a stone scuttling underfoot, he looked over at K. There was a distant look on her face and he found himself frowning. The urge to comfort her overwhelmed him and he shook his head, feeling momentarily confused. *No, it's Nora I love. Right?*

As they continued their travels, they sank ever deeper into their melancholy, the tenuous thread that held onto their mood steadily unraveling.

K chewed her lip. *Fine, he can go and be happy. He can just leave me alone.* That was how it was going to be anyway. She knew this! Hell, he hadn't stopped sniveling about that woman for four years! In a sudden moment of anger, she kicked hard at a rock in the path, sending it flying ahead of them. *It's fine, I'm used to being alone.*

Voltaire's hands were in his pocket and he didn't say anything. He was lost in thought as well, worrying over Penelope, his children. *It seems I just keep failing them.*

They were blessed with no storms, sleeping in the tents at night as they trudged along the roads. Their conversations were jovial as if everyone were trying to keep up the facade of everything being all right. Just before they reached the next town, though, the heavens opened up and down came a torrential downpour.

"Fitting, since this is really everyone's mood," Leon muttered as his hair became plastered to his face. Lilly shivered, looking as if someone had tossed her into a lake and pulled her back out. "Come on, everyone, it's not that far." Leon took the lead for a moment, knowing the way. He and Lilly had traveled to Chamberre many times by foot.

Quickening their pace, they entered the decent-sized town and began searching for the inn. It wasn't long before they found it. The place was small and slightly run-down but at the moment no one cared. All they wanted was to get out of the freezing rain.

Taking the lead again, since he was the man with the money, Voltaire entered the inn just as a gust of wind seemingly sent the rest of them tumbling into it. Finnegan shut the door with a bit of effort and shook himself off. A bard was strumming her lute and singing by the fireplace.

Local farmers and a few wanderers turned their heads for a moment but then returned to listening to the bard sing.

The large bald man behind the counter leaned forward, placing his elbows on the dark, aged wood and eyeing them suspiciously. "Well, my lucky day. Storm keeps bringing me paying customers...You are paying customers right?"

Taking a step forward, Voltaire leaned on the counter. "Of course, monsieur, we are paying customers. Do you have room to accommodate us?" He rolled a gold coin across his knuckles.

"Aye, I've got rooms for you, five gold apiece." He folded his arms as if daring Voltaire to barter with him.

Any other time, he might have, but right now he was cold and wet and just wanted to get this over with so that they could get to their rooms. "Of course." Counting out the gold, he handed it to the innkeeper, who gladly added it to his satchel.

"This way. I will show you your rooms." He pushed himself back from the counter, lifted the edge of the bar, and squeezed his way out. "A meal is included, whether it be dinner or breakfast." He lumbered toward a set of doors and opened them up. The group peered down the hall, which had four doors on each side. He pointed to the last two doors. "I only have two rooms, but they each have two beds. One of you shall have to share."

"Lilly can stay with me," Leon said, much to Lilly's annoyance. She never got any sleep with him because he was always rolling and stealing all the covers. They headed into a room with Voltaire while Finnegan and K took the room next door. Both parties were too exhausted to even think about food. All they wanted was to get out of their wet clothes and sleep.

Voltaire crawled into his bed in fresh dry clothes, turning his back to the twins. Lilly frowned, knowing that he was upset and that there was no way she could help him. Leon was already out like a light, as usual. Sighing, she lay on the bed, her back against her brother's. She was facing Voltaire, her gaze on him but her thoughts pulled inward.

Next door an awkward silence had fallen between Finnegan and K. Gone was their usual banter, their teasing remarks. Instead they mumbled their excuse me's when they bumped into each other, and their goodnights as they retreated to their beds. Each of them felt a bit lonely as they drifted off to sleep.

Leon was the first to wake, as usual. Moving carefully so as not to wake Lilly, he eased off the bed and made his way down the stairs where he was met by the innkeeper.

"Hungry, lad?" asked the innkeeper. His voice was surprisingly cheery compared to his tone the night before. Leon wondered for a moment if the man even slept. He was wearing the same clothes as the night before, the only difference being that his apron was a very pristine white.

"I am, in fact, though I should wait for the others." His stomach rumbled in protest.

"I think you have your answer. Sit, I'll bring you something to eat." The large man, rather spry for his size, dashed back to the kitchen.

Leon relented and sat down at a table. "Do you know where the livery is, possibly?" he asked once the innkeeper had returned with eggs, slices of ham, and toasted bread with honey.

"Just go out the door, take a right, and follow the road down. It's at the end of town. You looking to buy some horses?" He set down the plate of ham.

"Yes, hopefully they will have enough for us." Leon's mouth salivated at the sight of food. He was starving.

"They should. It's been slow this year, especially right now with the coming storms." The man tossed his towel over his shoulder and folded his arms.

Leon nodded in agreement. "Of all the times to head out to Gafton and the Twisted Forest." Taking a drink of warm milk, he dug into his meal.

"Now what in blazes would send you to the Twisted Forest?" There was surprise in his voice as well as horror.

"We're looking for amber. Tales say there is a tree surrounded by amber," Leon answered with his mouth full, then realized what he was doing and swallowed. "Sorry," he murmured.

"Don't even worry about it, I'm pleased you enjoy my food. Well, you had best be careful. Word has it the forest is haunted and if you stay in it too long bad things start to happen." The large man almost shivered at the idea.

Leon figured it wouldn't be anything easy, but hopefully it wasn't as bad as the innkeeper made it out to be.

It didn't take long for everyone to wake up and join Leon for breakfast. Their usual jovial bantering was absent as they ate. At the end of the meal, they left in silence toward the livery. Just as the innkeeper had predicted, there were plenty of horses to choose from.

They saddled up and took off. Now that they were moving on horse and not on foot, their timeline shrank greatly. Finnegan felt a mix of joy, excitement, and sadness as they rode closer and closer to Gafton.

K did her best to seem normal, but it was obvious she was upset. The dour mood clung to them as they continued their travels. Then, at last, they reached Gafton.

"I'll go ask around, Finnegan. Breathe, man." Voltaire smiled as they rode into town. Having gotten Nora's description from Finn, he headed to the first tavern he could find and dismounted. He went inside and began asking around. He soon found that Nora lived at the edge of town on a small farm.

He paused for a moment, thinking it strange. Finnegan had said she had been kidnapped... Perhaps she had escaped and settled here. He thought to mention it, but changed his mind, not wanting to further inflame the already emotionally charged group.

They gave him a quick description and Voltaire returned, mounting back up and motioning for the others to follow.

Off in the distance a small house with three tall trees beside it and a river running nearby started to appear. Just as Sephtis has scryed. Finnegan shook his head slightly and ran his fingers through his hair, trying to deal with the growing excitement, along with a rather large dash of fear. The small house grew bigger and bigger on the horizon as they steadily rode toward it, until at last they reached it. Finnegan looked back at K. "You will come with me, won't you?" K had been with him since the beginning.

"Of course I will." She nodded, ignoring the sudden feeling of despair as she dismounted. Voltaire climbed down from his mount as well, giving the reins to Leon. K had not necessarily been her carefree self. Despite her own attempts at ignoring her feelings for Finnegan, he was well aware and he wanted to be ready just in case that thin string holding her back snapped. The skies were clear and the air crisp. The sun's rays were beating down on them, but there was no warmth.

Finnegan grasped the box, made his way up to the door, and knocked. Questions ran through his mind as he tried to figure out what had happened to Nora and what was going to happen to her. What about K? What would happen to her once he left?

K kept a little behind, not wanting to crowd him. Her hands were tight fists, her eyes red and raw, but she refused any tears. Folding her arms, she looked away, not really wanting to see this woman who was taking her Finnegan away.

Moments later Finnegan heard footsteps, and then the door swung open and there she was. "Nora..." he breathed. He had finally found her. She was as lovely as ever with her blonde hair and sky blue eyes.

"Finnegan! What— What are you doing here?" the woman asked in complete surprise. Looking around she noticed the young woman slightly behind Finnegan, and a few steps from her, a roguish-looking man standing with his arms folded and two young adults on horseback.

"I have been looking for you since the day you were taken from me. I've spent the last four years doing whatever it took to find you and now...here you are!" He was expecting her to be thrilled, excited, happy to see him, but instead she looked upset.

"Why... I don't... Finnegan, I wasn't taken... I left..." Nora looked unashamed.

"YOU WHAT!?" K's voice boomed. "You left? Without a word you just left him?! He has loved you and looked for you all these years..." She was charging forward, seconds from tearing the woman apart, when Voltaire grabbed her waist. "Let me go!" she demanded as she struggled to free herself from Voltaire's grip. "You bitch!" she snarled at the woman.

"Let's go!" Voltaire pulled her back. Lilly jumped down to join the captain in trying to calm K, who was close to punching them both to get to Nora.

Finnegan remained standing at the front door in shock. "You left?" he said numbly. "Then why did you ever say yes to marrying me?" he blurted, using his anger to cover his pain. Pacing the front door, he stopped and stared at her when she began speaking again.

"I thought I wanted to marry you, but then I panicked. You are a noble, Finnegan! Your family was never going to accept me." Nora shook her head in confusion, her arms folded tightly to her chest. "Did you not get my letter? I told you all of this. Why did you come looking?"

"Letter? What letter?!" snapped Finnegan, glaring down at her with his hands on his hips.

"I left a letter with your brother Wilmud, and I left the ring," Nora explained. "He was supposed to give it to you. I told him I was leaving to go to Chamberre."

Finnegan took a step back as if he had been slapped in the face. He remembered that night so clearly. He had come home and Wilmud had been waiting for him, pacing the floor. Finnegan had been in such a good mood with is nuptials coming up in a few days' time.

"Wilmud! What are you doing here? Already have ideas for becoming my best man?" Finnegan had teased his younger brother.

"Finnegan, I have dire news. Nora was by the docks shopping this morning. We had a raid, marauders came... Finnegan, she was taken. I was able to find out the ship's name. I am so sorry." Wilmud had placed his hands on his brother's shoulders.

"No, no, this can't be! I have to find her, I have to go." Finnegan's voice had filled with panic.

"Father will never allow it, Finnegan. You can't! If you go, you forfeit your title, all of it. Think this through, brother, please!" Wilmud had begged him.

"No, I cannot, I will not leave her to that kind of fate!" he'd yelled.

But as his brother had said, his father had stripped him of his title, his money, and anything else that connected him to his family. Finnegan was no longer the heir.

Finnegan couldn't believe it... Wilmud had betrayed him. His own brother! For what? To become the heir? For prestige? All he knew was that he was going to find out.

"I am sorry for disturbing you, Nora," Finnegan said with a slight bow.

"I am as well, Finnegan," Nora said as her shoulders sagged and she shut the door.

Finnegan stalked back over to his horse and mounted up. "Let's get out of here," he scoffed and took off. When he found a place to make camp he dismounted and without a word began setting up his tent. He pounded the stakes in with hard heavy thuds, the metal clanging loudly. When he was done he dropped the mallet on the ground and stared off into the distance. He then went to wipe his hands on his breaches when he felt a hard object in his pocket. He pulled out the ring and stared at it for a while.

K slid off her horse and held onto the saddle to keep herself upright. Her legs felt like jelly, much like the rest of her. She glumly undid the saddle and tossed it to the side before finding some small comfort in brushing her steed. Once her horse was settled she turned to find Finnegan and saw the ring in his hand, then his red eyes. "That bitch!" she hissed and spun around to get her horse. Thoughts of beating that other woman within an inch of her life flashed through her mind.

Finnegan's lip flickered despite his pain. *K... Oh, shit, K.* He ran after her and grabbed her arms. K kicked him hard in the shin.

"Ow, son of a bitch..." Finnegan yelped in pain as her boots hit the mark.

"Oh gods, Finnegan, I'm sorry!" K spun around, surprise on her face. "I thought you were Voltaire!"

"Better you than me," Voltaire called with a smirk as he set up his tent.

"No, it's me—and where do you think you're going?" He rubbed his shin tenderly.

"I was... I was just..." Her voice trailed as her face turned red.

"Don't go, just stay with me." He sighed and rubbed his eyes, which stung from tears about to break free. "I need my friend." Finnegan proceeded to tell her all that Nora had said and that the others had overheard.

K's eyes widened and her once-tense body relaxed. "Of course, I can't believe— I'm so sorry."

The twins were finishing up their tent and overhearing the drama between K and Finnegan when Lilly finally stopped and declared, "I will cook something," then gazed over at Leon and motioned for him to talk to Finnegan.

Leon sighed and rolled his eyes when no one else was looking.

"Hey, Finnegan, let's go get some firewood for the fire," Leon offered. Finnegan was going to say no but nodded, as everyone else was working on something.

Despite being younger, Leon always had been a bit wiser than most. As they searched for branches from the sparsely planted trees, Leon quietly waited for the right moment to begin talking. When he thought they were far enough away from the others not to be overheard, he took his chance. "I know you're not okay and I can't even imagine what you are going through, but I promise you it's not as bad as it seems."

"Really? I can't really see how. I've spent the last four years searching for a woman I loved, only to find out she didn't get kidnapped. She left and my brother lied to me so that I would be stripped of my title and inheritance. Now I'm stuck with heartache and a ring I have no use for," he grumbled, adding another stick.

"Well, who did you meet during that time?" Leon asked, calmly gathering another stick.

"Sephtis...not a complete joy..." he muttered. "K." His voice softened.

Leon flashed a quick smile. "That's right, you met K, and wasn't she worth meeting?"

Finnegan sighed. Pausing from picking up the firewood, he shifted his weight, thought about the sly minx, and began to smile. "I can't imagine my life without her in it."

"Now tell me, were you really in love with Nora or just the fantasy you created? We often forget all the bad things and are left remembering only the good. Perhaps the love you feel is not love for Nora but for someone else." *You love K, you idiot,* part of him wanted to yell. *Open your eyes. Everyone sees it but you.* That same part of him wanted to say this to K as well, since she was just as blind.

"All right, let's head back." He had planted the thoughts in Finnegan's head. Hopefully they would take root and what had happened to him today would turn into a blessing.

Once back at camp they saw Lilly putting food into a small pot of water, as if planning to make a stew. "Just in time," she said, smiling and placing the pot on a makeshift holder. "All we need is the wood you brought and some fire." Finnegan quickly began setting up the wood underneath and adding some dry moss he'd found while Leon struck some flint and started a spark.

"Hopefully it will stay dry." Voltaire glanced up at the sky.

"It should. I don't see the storm clouds or smell the rain," Leon murmured before taking in a deep breath, enjoying the scent around him.

Finnegan was deep in thought. "I'm... I'm going to my tent," he murmured, turning abruptly and heading to his tent.

K watched him for a moment before following.

Lilly and Voltaire looked expectantly at Leon, who just shrugged, sat down on a blanket, and leaned against the saddle.

K kicked off her boots and sat down on her side of the tent. Finnegan sat on the other side frowning, his brow drawing together, relaxing, and then drawing back together. Leon's private words to him earlier that day were running through his head. Did he really just love the *idea* of Nora...the fantasy of being with her and living happily ever after with her? She didn't even seem real anymore, though the hurt he felt was real. Feeling movement, he looked next to him to see K. She wasn't looking at him, but rather staring at her fingers as she played with them. He smiled slightly at the memory of the first time he had met her. She had been laughing at his attempts to rescue her from a few hooligans, only to find out later that she had been swindling them. "I don't need rescuing, handsome," she had told him. "But you can buy me a drink." Between her smile, attitude, and soul-piercing eyes, he had been hooked.

Turning his head, he looked over at K and gently wrapped his arm around her. "My brother betrayed me. Nora left a note saying she couldn't marry me, even gave Wilmud the ring back. He lied to me all this time." Finnegan paused. He was about to add "wasted time," but then he looked at K and knew it wasn't a waste, would never be. "Thank you for always having my back, K... I'm lucky you're not like a girl... I mean...not that you aren't a girl..."

K couldn't help but giggle. He was never good with talking about his real emotions. "I know what you are trying to say." She leaned into him and felt his lips kissing the top of her head. She looked up at him and smiled. "You know it's going to be all right, don't you? I know it hurts, but it will be okay, I promise. When this whole thing with Sephtis is done, we can go find your brother and give him the shock of his life. I will fleece him of every single cent."

Finnegan stared down, his emotions everywhere, and before he could think, his lips touched hers like a feather and sparks ran down both their backs. Their private moment was abruptly cut off by Lilly bellowing, "Dinner's ready!!!"

They continued sitting as they were for another long moment before both pulling back in unison. "I suppose we should go," Finnegan murmured, and K nodded, blushing when her stomach rumbled.

Finnegan laughed and poked her belly. "I know that sound...you need to be fed."

K giggled and backed up. "Come on, let's get something to eat," she said, shoving her boots on and crawling out of the tent, followed by the noble pirate.

Everyone sat down and Lilly happily passed out bowls of food. "I hope you like it."

"Your cooking is amazing, Lilly. Of course we will like it," Voltaire said. He seemed not to be able to get enough of her cooking. Voltaire swore she added some sort of magic to it because he had been feeling healthier and stronger than ever before these past few days he'd been eating it.

Lilly's cheeks flushed red, and when Voltaire wasn't looking, Leon fanned her with a leaf, which she promptly snatched out of his hands seconds before Voltaire looked up again from his bowl.

Leon giggled, which only made her punch him before sitting down next to him.

"Did I miss something?" Voltaire asked curiously, to which Lilly vigorously shook her head no.

"No, no, just Leon being Leon," she grumbled.

For the first time on this trip everyone laughed and the tense, dark cloud that had been following them from the moment they had started out on his quest had gone. Well, except the tension between Finnegan and K, but that was tension of an entirely different kind. When it was time to sleep, everyone crawled into their tents. Finnegan and K pretended the almost-kiss hadn't happened, and both pretended not to be thinking about it.

"I don't know about you, but I'm exhausted," Finnegan sighed and flopped down on his side of the bed.

"Yeah, and my ass is killing me... I'm not looking forward to tomorrow." K crawled under her blankets.

Finnegan giggled and was about to make a joke about rubbing her ass, but thought it might be bad timing.

"I know you're thinking about rubbing my ass, Finnegan," she said, her voice muffled as she drifted.

"So if I say my ass is sore, you'll think about rubbing mine?" he giggled.

K giggled. "Shut up and go to sleep."

"Good night, minx,"

"Good night, noble pirate."

Chapter 14

They rode for three more days before they reached the edge of the Twisted Forest. The sun was starting to set, and having pushed the horses a bit hard the last few hours, they all agreed to stop, take care of the horses, and set up camp. Lilly used a bit of her magic to help refresh the steeds while K and Finnegan began brushing them down. Leon and Voltaire took care of getting the camp set up. Night began to fall. They were too exhausted to really even think or talk, but that didn't stop them from their usual banter before bed.

The following morning they stood before the forest. "Wow..." Finnegan stared at the dead and Twisted Forest before them. "I mean, this is bad! Is there even a way through?" There was no color to the trees. They were pale—a mix of gray and white—and the bushes and vines were black as coal. The whole place seemed unnatural, eliciting involuntary shivers from everyone present.

"There's a reason I brought an axe." Leon drew out the axe and prepared to use it to slash away at the bizarre vegetation. Looking at how much there was to cut through, though, he wasn't sure the axe would be enough.

Lilly's chest tightened and an ache filled her. She could feel magic in these woods—and pain, so much pain. "I'm not sure that's the way, brother," she said, suddenly worried. What misfortune might befall them for bringing violence upon the forest?

"I don't think we have a choice, Lilly." Voltaire tilted his head as he tried to see some way through.

"There is always a choice." Lilly walked toward the forest and K stared into it. K was pale. She dreaded going in, but kept the feeling to herself. She had overheard Leon talking about how the forest revealed one's fears. K had spent years getting over the trauma that had been inflicted upon her in her youth. It was trauma she never wanted to remember, much less relive.

Lilly stood in front of the twisted, colorless vines that held a strangle hold on the lifeless trees. She could feel an ache deep within her like a small seed in her heart that implanted within her as she reached out tentatively, her fingers brushing against a small branch. She didn't know any actual spells, having learned magic only by feeling and focusing her will. She took in a breath, wrapped her hand gently around the branch, and, doing her best to ignore the suffocating anguish that bloomed within her, tried to impart her healing energy into it. Much to her delight the branches began to pull back and make way for them. With a smile she looked back at the group and began making her way into the forest.

"Does anyone else feel like this is a bad idea?" K muttered, clenching her fist as her eyes darted about like those of a cornered animal.

"We don't have a choice." Finnegan looked at her and became slightly worried. There was something in her demeanor he had not seen before. Fear.

"No, no, we don't," Voltaire admitted and followed Lilly and Leon.

Leon kept his axe near him just in case.

K stayed back for just a moment while the others entered the forest one by one. At last she took a deep breath, let it go, and made her own way inside. "Does anyone have any idea where this tree is?" she called, looking around and moving closer to Finnegan.

"The heart of the forest...that's what Lilly said was in the stories," Finnegan told her.

"Great," she muttered nervously when she felt a warm firm hand grasp hers. Relaxing some, she squeezed Finnegan's reassuring hand and moved closer to him.

No one knew how many hours they had been walking or even whether they had been walking toward the tree or just in circles. Lilly was getting exhausted because of how much of her energy it was taking to move away the branches. Leon worried over how much longer she could keep this up. When she stumbled, he called for a halt.

"You okay, Lilly?" Leon grabbed her arm and helped her up.

"I am. I just need a break." She rubbed her brow with her scuffed-up hands.

They circled up, sat down, took out canisters of water, and began drinking from them.

"I feel like we should have left a trail," Voltaire mused, looking behind him.

"Yeah...I agree," Finnegan sighed and leaned back against a fallen log.

K sat close to him. The forest unnerved her in a way nothing else did.

"Should we just camp here?" Voltaire asked, looking at the pale Lilly.

"I think that's a good idea," Leon said, nodding in agreement.

They did their best to set up a makeshift camp and huddled close to the small fire they had made. It was an uneasy night's rest.

There came a moment when all of them were fast asleep except Lilly, who kept hearing someone calling. Slipping out of Leon's embrace while still half asleep, she followed the voice.

"I'm coming..." she called back softly. Stumbling over limbs and rocks, the young mage suddenly fell into a clearing. Instead of hard rock, broken limbs, and dirt under her feet, there was soft, lush green grass. Her eyes widened as she looked up at the massive tree, which was surrounded by thousands of pieces of amber.

The disembodied ethereal voice spoke to her. "Welcome, child. You are the first to enter my domain with a pure heart intent on healing. Yet I sense you seek something else."

Lilly had an overwhelming sense of awe... This voice, it was... It was divine. It had to be. Kneeling down in reverence, she clasped her hands together. "I do...I am in need of a piece of amber...for...for my friend Voltaire."

"Ahhh, your heart holds love for this one. The path which you are on is dangerous, child. See what dark magic has wrought upon my precious forest, and only this small piece I have recovered? Though intent may be pure and filled with love, it can lead to darkness." The warning was clear to Lilly. But that did not water down her resolve.

"I understand. I promise to keep watch and make sure no darkness ensues," Lilly said firmly.

"I believe you... Come take the pieces that you need." The wind rushed around the young mage, pushing her toward the tree. Her pure heart was rewarded.

Lilly smiled and headed toward the tree. She took three pieces of amber and slipped them in her pocket. "Thank you, spirit. I will do my best to heal more along the way."

"To do that you will need to sleep. Rest upon this sacred ground and your energy will be renewed." An overwhelming need to sleep overcame her and she lay down on the soft, inviting grass and fell asleep.

Back in the forest Leon awoke to find Lilly gone.

He jumped up yelling "LILLY!" and everyone jerked awake and scrambled to their feet.

"What happened?" Voltaire shouted angrily, trying to hide the fear rising in his chest.

"I don't know," said Leon. "I just woke up and she was gone! LILLY!"

There was no response and panic was palpable among the group.

"Let's split up and try to find her," Finnegan said, to which the others agreed.

"Finnegan, stay close, won't you!" K said nervously.

"I will, K," Finnegan told her calmly.

"Keep within shouting distance," Leon called as they began scouring the forest for clues.

K, trying to keep calm, focused on looking for footsteps, broken branches—anything that might show the direction Lilly had gone. She moved farther away from camp, following what she thought were Lilly's footprints, when a pair of black boots appeared in front of her. Swallowing slowly, she followed the boots up to royal breeches, royal coat, and then the face that had long brought her nightmares.

"AHHHHHHH!!!" K screamed and tried to run when the apparition grabbed her.

"Don't you run from me!!" the familiar voice yelled.

"NO! NO! Get off of me! Get away from me!" Her screams turned to cries and sobs as she thrashed and flailed.

Finnegan had started running the second he'd heard her screaming. When he found her the image of the King attacking her confused him, but he didn't hesitate. Rushing toward the figure, he attempted to slam him down on the ground only to find himself passing through the figure and hitting the tree behind it, then reeling backward onto the ground. He shook his head to stop the spinning and scrambled up. Looking around, he saw only K, who had collapsed to the ground shaking and crying. The image of the King had disappeared.

"K..." He knelt next to her and placed his hands carefully on her. She flinched, then jerked, but he didn't let her go. "Hey, hey, it's me, it's okay."

K grabbed hold of Finnegan and buried her face in his chest, hiding her tears. Moments later the other two arrived.

"Everything okay?" Voltaire asked, seeing K shaking.

"It will be once we get out of here," Finnegan said.

"We are not leaving without my sister," Leon barked.

"No one is saying that," Captain said, calming the large man down.

There was a sudden burst of light and from it a stumbling Lilly emerged. Blinking, she looked around and saw K. "Oh, no, what happened?!"

Finnegan jerked to look up at Lilly, his eyes throwing daggers. "Forest showed her worst fear," he snarled. "Where were you?"

"Hey, don't snap at my sister!" Leon demanded, both men's hackles up.

Holding her hands up in a placating gesture, Lilly implored, "Easy, the both of you. I was at the tree of tears and I got the amber. Now let's get out of here. Just follow me." Much to everyone's surprise, she took the lead.

True to her word, Lilly healed as much as she could until they emerged at the same spot where they had entered. Then she turned to K and frowned. "I am so sorry, K, if I caused this."

"No, it's not your fault," K told her with a voice cracking from exhaustion. "In fact, you did it—you got the amber and got us out of here. You are the hero."

"Come on, let's saddle up and get as far away from this place as we can," Finnegan said with a strained voice. "I think we can all agree on that."

They passed Gafton as quickly as they could, making a wide berth around Nora's house. They wanted to get rid of that memory as well as the darkness before. Soon they found themselves in the town of Lorren. It was easy to see the inn as they loped into town. It was the largest building in town with an painted mural of what looked like a drunken man with a goat standing on him while he was sleeping on a bed a bit too small for him. The Drunken Goat looked inviting to the weary travelers.

A stable boy appeared when they rode up. "Take your horses?" he piped with a slight whistle, auburn hair sticking every which way as he smiled with a big smile that was missing a front tooth.

"Yeah, that would be great." Leon dismounted and handed the kid his reins. The others dismounted and tied their horses up while Voltaire gave him coin to take care of them. When they entered the inn there was a large fire burning. The place was moderately filled with talking and laughing patrons.

"You lot look as if you need a drink and sleep desperately," the innkeeper, Jones, called out to them.

"You would be right, sir...and we could all use a bath," Voltaire sighed and began counting out coin. He would need to get more soon.

"We've got some nice tubs in our lower rooms. How many do you need?" The wiry man's thin brow rose as he waited.

"Three." Leon spoke quickly.

Voltaire shrugged. "Three it is."

"Well, you are in luck. Have a drink and get warmed up while we get the baths ready," Jones said, pointing at the table by the fire.

They did as they were told and each was given a mug of mead. They drank silently, dirty and exhausted but feeling a bit victorious. They had scratched one item off Sephtis's list.

Glancing over at K and Finnegan, Voltaire couldn't help but smirk. Part of him wanted to make a bet to see how long it would take before they gave in to each other.

Sitting in silence they waited patiently for the innkeeper to return and let them into their rooms. By the time their drinks were done their rooms were ready and the Innkeeper handed them each a key. "Your rooms are just down this hall, hot baths ready for you."

"Thank you." Lilly smiled happily, getting up and taking the key.

Voltaire was eager to get to his room and get a bath. He felt like there was sand everywhere.

Finnegan walked with K into the room. "Take your bath first, K, okay? Try and relax." He rubbed her back, ignoring her flinching.

K nodded, headed over to the large tub, and began undressing. Sliding into the hot water, she sighed, wrapping her arms around her legs. "Will you join me?" Her voice was soft and hopeful.

He froze for a moment—the barrier that held them apart now gone—but then shook it off. He needed her right now as a friend. "Of course, minx." He walked over, pulled off his clothes, and kicked off his boots. Stepping into the hot tub, he groaned. "My muscles feel better already." Leaning back, he stretched his legs out and settled them on either side of her.

"I... That man... It's... I can't." Her throat tightened and she trembled. She hadn't felt such fear and vulnerability since she was fifteen. She hated the feeling. She had spent many years now making sure she never felt that way again, and now, in the blink of an eye, the forest had taken away her years of heard-earned confidence and calm.

"Hey, hey..." He reached out and grabbed her hands. "It's all right. You don't have to tell me, and don't worry... There is nothing you could ever do that would stop me from... from being your friend. You know that, right? Nothing." He wiped away the tears running down her cheeks. "Now turn around." He waited patiently as she slowly turned her back to him. "Close your eyes and just relax." The pirate began rubbing her neck and shoulders, lazily talking about anything and everything, until the emotionally exhausted K eventually fell asleep.

With ease he got her out of the tub and, wrapping a sheet around her, carried her to their bed. He tucked her in and wrapped himself protectively around her. He ached inside every time he saw the distressed look on her face. He swore to himself that he would find a way to make her smile again.

K woke up to her face pressed tightly into Finnegan's well-sculpted chest, their bodies tightly intertwined as she clung to him and he held her protectively. The small hairs on his chest tickled her nose and she lifted her face, giggling, until it was resting on his shoulder, her lips by his neck. She kept still because she didn't want to wake him, not yet. She felt safe like this. She stayed quiet, enjoying the moment, until finally Finnegan began to stir.

Lifting his head slightly and looking down at the woman wrapped tightly in his arms, he reveled in the feel of her soft, shapely body nestled snugly against his. She had such smooth skin and he couldn't help but notice those amazing breasts of hers that were pressed against his chest and making his breath quicken. He moved his free hand slowly up from behind her back, then gently down the curve of her hip, then behind her back again. Her body gave a slight tremor.

"I felt you giggling." His voice was sleepy and he purred slightly, placing his free hand on the bed and pushing himself up. He hovered slightly above her.

"Your chest hairs tickled my nose." Was it really warm all of a sudden? Her heart was thundering a little faster.

"Did they?" he teased, leaning down all of sudden and breathing her in. "You still smell like berries."

"I take it you like it?" Her body shifted slightly to get more comfortable. The subtle movements of skin gliding against skin sent jolts of excitement through both of them, making both their eyes flash for a moment.

"I do," he said softly.

"Finn..." She wasn't able to continue talking because his lips consumed hers with such passion that any thought was erased from her mind except for the need to match his passion with her own. His arms wrapped around her his fingers, curled deep into her hair. He shifted his body so that he was hovering above her, resting slightly on top of her. Then, suddenly, they both froze at the sound of footsteps rushing to their door.

They heard banging on the door and Voltaire's voice bellowing "WE GOTTA GO!"

Finnegan groaned and sat up. "This isn't over, minx." His voice was a mix of a growl and a purr.

K couldn't speak, which was strange for her. All she could do was nod as she got her clothes on.

Voltaire was still banging on the door when Finnegan reached it and jerked it open. "What is it?" he yelled, still wearing only his breeches.

Voltaire moved to the side, shoved Leon and Lilly through the door, and rushed them past Finnegan. Following quickly after, he grabbed the door from Finnegan and shut it behind him. "I don't know how, but it's been found out that Lilly got amber from that damn tree and now they are coming for her." Voltaire began barricading the door. "We need to jump out of the window."

The room was on the ground level so they wouldn't have far to jump. Leon rushed to the window and there was no latch to open it. They could hear a cacophony of angry voices and the door being slammed into. Leon grabbed a chair and threw it through the window, which burst outward in a shower of glass. Most of the glass rained down to the ground below, but some shards remained lodged in the frame. Leon frantically began breaking these away.

K took the blanket and tossed it over the window frame's bottom edge, covering some of the sharp edges. "Come on!" Grabbing Lilly's hand, she pulled the frightened girl through the window, quickly followed by the others.

Voltaire was just about to jump through when the door exploded open and an angry mob of men began rushing toward him. He hastily made his way through the window frame, and his feet hit the ground on the other side before the mob had been able to close the distance.

"Sorry, chaps, not this time... In fact, not ever." He winked and followed the rest of the group into the alleyway.

"This is our territory," Leon said, straightening up his shoulders.. "Follow us."

The street kids moved deftly through the back alleys, heading toward the forest. They could hear the men looking for them as they took a breath to collect their thoughts just inside the trees.

"This forest is smaller than the town—they will eventually find us," said Lilly, her voice strained and shaking.

"Nothing is going to happen to you, Lilly!" Voltaire promised vehemently. The young girl just nodded wide-eyed.

"Look, our best bet is to just keep moving and avoid the roads," said K, her hand on her blade and her eyes shifting constantly.

"K's right," Finnegan sighed, still frustrated at being interrupted. "If we stop now they will find us out of sheer dumb luck."

"All right, enough of this chatter. Let's go!" Leon grabbed Lilly's hand and took off, pulling her behind him.

Chapter 15

As the days passed, K could not shake the feeling they were being followed. Neither could Voltaire, which meant he stuck close to Lilly. Not that she minded.

They were only one night away from reaching port and the group agreed to lie outside to keep close. Everyone had fallen asleep except Voltaire. He heard something in the woods and his bright blue eyes flashed. He was going to stop this person once and for all. Closing his eyes, he pretended to be sleeping.

The stranger moved closer to Lilly. This was his chance—everyone was sleeping. The stranger was so focused on Lilly he never noticed the figure moving behind him until it was too late. Voltaire grabbed the back of the man's head and with one swift move slit his neck so deep warm wet blood gushed out all over Lilly, waking her.

Lilly saw the stranger collapse and then saw a fountain of blood wash over her body and Voltaire's hands. She trembled slightly but did not scream. She had been inured to the sight of blood and death, having grown up on the streets. She quickly rose, grabbed her pack, took Voltaire's hands, and headed to the small nearby stream. This wasn't even the first time she'd had to deal with a dead body. Leon had killed before to keep her safe and she had seen the carnage and dealt with the aftermath.

"Are you all right?" she asked, pushing Voltaire down to the ground and taking off her bloodied dress. She soaked it in the stream and then used it to wash off Voltaire's hands.

"I'm fine." His voice was terse. "Are you?"

"I'm fine, Voltaire. I have you and Leon to protect me." Her voice was soft and calming as she felt his hands loosen their grip on her.

"You should put a new dress on, Lilly," he murmured softly. "It's cold out."

Lilly nodded, put her dress on, and then felt Voltaire put his long coat over her already-jacketed upper body.

"Here, wear this till you warm up," he said. The thick coat was well treated and wiping off the blood was easy.

Voltaire rolled up his sleeves and walked Lilly back to the campsite. He shook his head at the others, who were still passed out sleeping. They had been running hard, so it was not too surprising. "Go ahead and lay on my bed," he told Lilly as he walked over to the corpse. He grabbed the dead man's legs and began dragging him away. The sound of nearby wolves and scavengers sent a slight chill up his spine, but he figured why not let them feast on the corpse of their failed attacker. The bastard deserved nothing less. Dropping his legs, he began heading back to camp, and he could hear the sounds of flesh being torn.

Lilly had fallen asleep, and Voltaire sat down next to the fire and tossed a few more pieces of wood onto it. As the sun began to rise, he fell asleep slightly, only to be woken by Leon's panic as he saw the massive blood stain where his sister had been sleeping.

"Leon, she is over here," Voltaire said, motioning behind him.

"What happened?" Leon asked, still trying to calm down.

"The stranger showed up and I took care of him before he could hurt Lilly." Voltaire shrugged. Finnegan and K both woke to hear Voltaire say he had taken care of the guy chasing them.

"Well, at least we don't have to run anymore," Finnegan said sitting up.

It was a month of board games and wine as they traveled the seas to the old country. They were docking before the sun even began to peak. Voltaire barked his instructions and the men scrambled to get things done, eager to explore this world. Many of them had only worked the simple trade routes, so this was a new experience for them.

Finnegan was struggling with his desire, but the ship wasn't the most romantic place to be with a woman. Not with twenty other pirates eagerly wanting to listen in. K, though, was getting more and more frustrated with him ignoring her and not even being willing to speak about the kiss they had shared.

Leon and Lilly were dressed and ready to begin searching. Lilly was excited. Finally, Voltaire would be able to see his children.

The group made its way down the dock to the harbormaster. Voltaire rushed over to him. "Excuse me, do you have a ship called the *Mermaid's Quest* docked here?"

The old man looked through his books. "Aye, I did, but she just left yesterday."

"DAMN IT!" Voltaire exploded. The desire to punch someone or something was so overwhelming Voltaire forced himself to walk way before he caused a scene.

Lilly frowned but stepped forward. "Did they sell any children here for service?"

"Aye, they did, a few. The auction is in the middle of town." The harbormaster pointed.

"Thank you!" Lilly rushed over to Voltaire and grabbed his hand. "Voltaire, come on, they said there were some children sold. They are having an auction."

Voltaire looked over to where she was pointing and nodded. "Let's go!"

With determination they headed toward the heart of the city. As they drew nearer they could hear the auctioneers calling people to come up and get ready to purchase the newest children to arrive.

"I can't believe this is real," K said, watching as people gathered around the large stage, holding out their coin purses and talking amongst themselves.

"It's disgusting is what it is," Finnegan spat, folding his arms across his chest.

"Will he even know what his kids look like?" Leon whispered.

"I have no idea," muttered K.

Meanwhile Voltaire, with Lilly in hand, made his way toward the tent where the children were being held. As they approached, two large guards stood watch like hawks over the entrance.

"I just want to take a closer look at the merchandise," said Voltaire. He shook a rather large purse and the men glanced at each other and nodded. Rushing past them, he began calling out his daughter's names. A few girls rushed to the front, crying and reaching their hands out, but as he looked he was deflated to see that none of them were his girls.

"They aren't here, Lilly..." His voice began to break. "They aren't here."

Lilly squeezed his hand. "Don't worry, Voltaire, we will find them, I promise."

With sagging shoulders he left the tent of screaming and crying children. Lilly frowned, wrapping her arm around his. "This is horrible. I wish we could save them."

"I'm sorry, Lilly," he said, his voice thick with emotion. He reached the others and they looked at him hopefully, but he shook his head.

"Don't worry, Voltaire," said Finnegan, trying to be encouraging. "We can have Sephtis scry for them. If he found Nora, he can find your kids."

K stiffened at the sound of Finnegan saying Nora's name.

"Let's just get out of here," Voltaire muttered. "This place is making me sick."

The skies looked dark up ahead as the ship set sail. The crew was unsure of whether it would be best to go straight through the gathering storm or head around it. Voltaire put it up for a vote and the crew chose to go through. They kept watch as the days passed and the sky grew darker and darker until the storm was upon them. The men knew what to do, and Voltaire shouted a few orders and warnings as they navigated the tempest.

Leon told Lilly to stay in the cabin while he and K went out to help the crew. One of the men wasn't paying attention when a swell knocked him off his feet. Leon and K scrambled to grab him, but he slipped through their hands and went into the water. Those who could rushed over to try to get him out. They almost had him when a dark tentacle slipped out of the water, wrapped around his waist, and pulled him under.

"GET BACK!" Voltaire roared when he saw the creature rising from the water. A chill went through him as its shinning bulbous head turned to regard the men with one of its vast baleful eyes. Gripping the wheel, he did his best to veer the ship away from the fearsome visage. "THROW WHATEVER BOXES WE HAVE OVERBOARD!!" Voltaire ordered.

The men began grabbing and throwing boxes and anything else they could find in hopes of distracting the sea monster that seemed intent on dragging them to the murky depths. Its slithering tentacles grasped and pulled the ship, causing it to list to one side and the men and gear to slide across the deck toward the water. The beast became distracted and released its hold, shifting its attention to the falling boxes as they floated and bobbed in the water.

The plan had worked and they were able to get just enough distance between them and the monstrosity. The crew let out a sigh of relief, and the storm began to lighten to a soft patter, as if the heavens felt they had dealt enough wrath.

Leon and K checked on the men, and the ship then reported back to Voltaire, who nodded his thanks, his lips pulled into a tight frown. As the sea settled Voltaire called all hands on deck and asked Leon to bring up a keg of ale. Cracking it open, he passed out a mug to each member of the crew.

"I want us to take a moment to remember Danny," he said. "Always one with the quick wit and a joke. He worked hard and played even harder. He was a good lad. May he reach the lady's embrace

102

swiftly." He raised his mug and everyone let out a resounding cheer, downed their drinks, and quickly went to refill their mugs.

When they finally reached the mansion everyone was in a foul mood. Sephtis opened the door to see the solemn bunch making their way up to him.

"You took your time." He folded his arms and his eyes darkened, causing the clouds to darken and the thunder to sound. His mood often held sway to the island's weather when it was particularly intense.

"Give us a break, Sephtis," K protested. "This has been a shitty run. We were only a bit longer than usual. We got what you wanted. Isn't that enough?"

"Enough, Double K!" he snarled at her. The nickname held the power of a dark secret that K had done her best to hide—that she would do anything to hide.

K's face dropped and she turned white as a sheet. "I... I..."

"Get inside, all of you." Sephtis tossed the doors open and made his way inside. "Now where is the amber?"

Lilly nervously reached into her pocket, not really wanting to give the amber tears to the man. But if it helped Voltaire... Sephtis spun around and snatched the pieces from her hand.

"Excellent. Take your rest. I have your new destination already plotted out." Sephtis headed to his laboratory, followed by Voltaire.

Lilly frowned and looked over at Leon, who shook his head. "I'm heading to bed," he said. Taking one last look in Voltaire's direction, Lilly followed Leon up the stairs.

K had gone to the large library and the cabinet that held all of the strong liquor. Grabbing a crystal decanter and a glass, she filled it up, drank the liquor down, and then refilled the glass. Turning around, she tossed the glass and its contents into the fire.

"K?" Finnegan asked, stepping in just as the flames surged and roared from their newfound fuel source.

"What?" Her voice was flat as she sat in the large black leather wingback chair.

"Are you all right?" Finnegan made his way to her and sat down on the footstool in front of her.

"I'm fine. You don't need to worry about me." She stared into the fire, her fingers running along a crack on the chair's armrest.

"Right, you seem just as happy as ever," he retorted, sounding just as snappy.

Hazel eyes flashed as she glared at him. "What do you know about happy?"

"I know I am happy when I'm with you." His voice held conviction and his eyes were soft and adoring.

"You...what?" She shook her head, trying not to smile despite her mood.

"I am happy with you... In fact, it's the only time I'm really happy." He took her hands and gently kissed them.

"I am too," K whispered.

Tilting her chin up, Finnegan kissed her sweetly, enjoying the feel of her soft lips on his. K ran her fingertips along his jaw and down his neck, feeling his pulse jump as she did so. Finnegan stood and with one swift motion picked her up and held her close to him.

As he went to take her out of the room, the door opened up. "Ah, there you two are," said Sephtis. "Come with me."

Finnegan's head fell back and he groaned in irritation. "Seriously, now?"

"Yes, now...put her down. You can carry her over the threshold some other time."

With a heavy sigh, Finnegan put K down and followed Sephtis to his laboratory, where Voltaire was staring at a map and plotting their destination.

"Why do you need us, Sephtis?" Finnegan's voice was on edge. "Because I need to give you information. Before you were going into some forest..."

K interrupted, "It was a horrible forest, Sephtis."

"Whatever. This scrying mirror belongs to a powerful mage by the name of Rune Lordan. He lives in the Forgotten Deserts behind Ahris. Apparently he couldn't deign to live amongst the common people and built up his own fortress. I think there may be some trouble getting in, since he has guards. I don't think talking will go over well, but you may be able to sneak in and steal it."

"Fine, sounds great. We have time to come up with a plan," Finnegan grumbled. Grabbing K's hand, he pulled her out of the laboratory.

Giggling, she followed him as he pulled her quickly up the stairs. "Finn, I don't think he was done."

"Oh, he was done," Finnegan said, throwing open the door to his room and pulling her inside. He slammed the door shut and shoved K up against it. His lips claimed hers hungrily and he tore at her clothes. When their lips parted K gasped slightly and began pulling up Finnegan's tunic. Once she had worked it off, she flung it hastily to the ground. She kissed him hard, her hands traveling down each ridge of his chest before her fingers began unlacing his breeches as she kicked off her boots.

Their hands caressed, scratched, and mapped each other's bodies as they made their way to the bed, discarding the rest of their clothing. Reaching the edge, Finnegan pushed her onto the bed, moaning softly at the feel of her below him. He had fooled himself for so long—wasted time—but no more. His rough hands slid across her supple body with demanding hunger as he crawled eagerly on top of her. His lips claimed hers possessively before traveling down her neck and collarbone as he wrapped his arm underneath her and pulled her up and over so she was lying gently on the pillows. His hand found hers and his fingers intertwined with her fingers and held them firmly as he continued teasing her with kisses, nips, and flicks of his tongue.

K ran her fingers through his hair as his lips ran down her chest, finally reaching her breasts. Indulging himself, he eagerly ran his tongue along her already dusky pink nipple while his other hand fondled her soft sumptuous breast. The pirate was even more pleased when a gasp followed by a moan left K's lips. Smiling, he switched sides—it was important to give equal attention.

At the sound of her gasping yet again, his lips trailed down her stomach, kissing and biting her skin. When he reached her navel, her body was quivering. Excitement and nervous desire were rushing through both of them, and as much as Finnegan's body was screaming at him to mount her and claim her as his, he bit back and kissed down her hips and thighs, which he was pleased to find parting for him. Without hesitation he buried his face between her legs, his strong tongue eagerly exploring her soft folds and that soft bundle of nerves, making her gasp loudly.

"Oh, gods, Finn..." K panted. Her hips rolled and her hands dug into the sheets.

Redoubling his efforts, he held her ass like it was a plate and he was a man starving. Her body shivered. "Finn... Finn, if you don't stop..." she gasped, feeling her body tense up.

"We've got all night," he purred, still going.

K's body arched. "Oh, gods... Yes!" she cried out as her body locked up in orgasmic bliss. After lapping up her excitement, he kissed her thighs and hips and began a trail of kisses back up to her lips.

He throbbed with excitement as he settled between her legs. "K..." he moaned, pressing against her, giving her a moment to reconsider. His answer was her hands on his lower back pulling him toward her. Without hesitation he immersed himself in her to the hilt, moaning and growling in pleasure. As he thrust deeply into her, the two of them moaned in unison.

Finnegan knew without a doubt that he loved this little minx underneath him. He knew he had loved her from the very beginning. He had just been too lost in his own private obsession to clearly see it. But not any more. K was his and was going to stay his. He planned to make sure of it.

Their bodies rocked and ground against each other as they growled and cried out in pleasure. Any fineness of lovemaking gave way to a primal greediness as they careened into each other with a force known only to lovers of passion. As they grew closer and closer to their peaks, their movements became faster, harder, greedier as they groped and caressed each other into a sexual frenzy.

"That's it... Yes, FINN!" K's legs and arms tightened around him as wave after wave of ecstasy washed over her. Finn, unable to hold on any longer, pumped hard into K until he was spent and sent her into another wave of orgasmic bliss.

Gasping for breath, Finnegan lay gently on K, their bodies wet with sweat. K kissed Finnegan's lips and eyes. "We are definitely doing that again," she said, still breathless.

"Like I said..." he said, claiming her lips and biting them playfully, "We have all night and all day."

Chapter 16

Voltaire sat in the large chair in the library, drowning his pain in glasses of whisky. The cries of his wife and children were screaming at him, demanding why he had not saved them.

Down the stairs Sephtis stared at the body of Penelope. She was beautiful and reminded him of his Layla. If this worked...if he could do this, then there was hope for others whose loved ones had been taken from them before their time. How long had he researched, tried, and failed at this? But he knew he was on the right path. He could feel it in his bones and he would let nothing get in his way.

Voltaire had been right about Finnegan and K—they didn't emerge from their bedroom for three days. Servants brought them food and drink, but they had everything they needed in their bedroom.

Lilly kept busy getting supplies ready for the trip. Sometimes she was accompanied by Voltaire, who would sit and watch her while his thoughts drifted to his wife and children.

Leon found himself in Sephtis's armory looking at the vast trove of weapons. He found a nice pair of axes and began working with them. He had some axe-fighting skills as well as natural talent.

When it was time to leave, Leon wasn't sure which was worse, Finnegan and K not realizing they loved each other...or them now knowing and groping each other when they thought no one was looking.

Finnegan followed K into her cabin. "I think this is going to be the first fun trip I've had on a ship," he purred at her, tugging at her corset.

K batted away his hand. "You are insatiable..." she giggled. "Yes, I think it will be fun." She grabbed his ass playfully before jumping away from him.

"I'm not the only one who is insatiable." He shoved her playfully onto the bed, crawling on top of her.

"Finn..." she laughed, trying to push him off. "I have work to do."

"Leon can take care of it," he said, claiming her lips eagerly.

Whatever resistance she'd had earlier now melted away and she pulled him down and wrapped her legs around him.

Outside the door Leon rolled his eyes at the sounds the two of them made.

"What's with the eyeroll?" Lilly asked as Voltaire walked by and paused.

They were rewarded with gasps and growls.

"Ugh," the twins replied as Voltaire shrugged and made his way back to his cabin.

It took them over a month to travel back to Ahris. When they docked, K wanted to check out everything first, make sure that soldiers were no longer looking for Merrin Blackmoor.

She returned with a big smile on her face. "We are in luck! They stopped looking for you some time ago. They presume you are dead!"

"Well, that is good news." Voltaire nodded. "Did you get the horses we needed?" He walked down the plank, followed by Leon and Lilly.

"Yes, Finnegan is with them now. We are ready to go. It should only take us a few days to get to the desert. I even packed a few costumes just in case." She smiled wide—a bit of a surprising sight for them.

"Well, let's get moving, then." Voltaire motioned for K to lead the way.

Finnegan was standing near the docks holding the reins of the horses. They were snorting and stamping their feet, seemingly as eager to get moving as were their soon-to-be riders.

"There you guys are. We should get going. I hear this mage is no piece of cake and we will need time to strategize." Finnegan handed everyone their horses and helped K up on hers before mounting up himself.

"What have you heard?" Voltaire asked as they headed out.

"Rune's place is well guarded by not just mercenaries but summoned creatures. We are going to need to fight our way through probably..." He looked over at Leon. "But I think with the three of us we should be fine." Finnegan smirked.

"All right, we will see." Voltaire looked over at Lilly. She was no fighter; he had to make sure she was safe. He would never forgive himself if anything happened to her. He had already failed his wife and kids. He couldn't let another fall under his care.

Leon was thinking the same thing as he anxiously regarded Lilly, who was looking at the map and planning their path. "Did it seem like Sephtis knew this mage?" Leon shifted his gaze to Voltaire and K.

"I heard him speak of him once. Rune was to be the next archmage in the mages' guild of Ahris but was passed over. Apparently he quit the guild in such a spectacular fashion he was banned from it. I asked him what it was he did and Sephtis just smiled and said nothing. Just that he wished he had done something as dramatic when they kicked him out in Chamberre." K shrugged. "But beyond that, nothing."

"Great," Finnegan groaned. "A mage with a chip on his shoulder, as if we don't have enough of those."

"We should get going," Lilly called out to the group, rolling up the leather map Sephtis had given her. "We've got quite a ways to go before we reach the desert."

"Of course he lives there," Leon snorted. "He's probably as dry and salty as the sand." Leon hated the desert. The very idea of having to traipse through the sand made him angry.

"Don't mind Leon. Last time we were in a desert, we almost didn't make it out. He's still sensitive about it." Lilly smiled slightly.

"With good reason," Leon snapped. "We almost died."

"But we didn't," said Lilly. "Now let's go. No time to waste."

Voltaire smiled as Lilly easily took the lead and everyone fell in step.

As they crossed the border separating green lands from the dry desert, they were struck by how suddenly one transitioned to the other.

"Nothing screams you're going to have a slow long death like a horizon full of sand," Finnegan quipped.

"Tell me we brought enough water." Voltaire smirked at Finnegan.

"I hope so, but who knows how long we are going to be out there."

"Don't worry, there are ways to find water even in the desert." Lilly smiled encouragingly.

K shifted her weight on the saddle and patted her paint's neck. "Well, there is a stream not too far back. We could always go back and fill up just to be safe. Two of us could go and do it."

"Oh, no, no, we are not letting you two go," Leon grumbled. "We won't see you for a week. I'll go with the captain."

K's eyes widened and Finnegan started laughing. "Well, he is right, K."

"Oh, shut up." Her lips pulled back into a slight smile. "All right, go. It won't take but a few hours. We will set up camp here."

As K had predicted, it took about four hours for the two to get to the stream and return, having filled every container they had. Voltaire even poured out a bottle of fine whiskey to fill it with water, though he cursed the entire time.

When they woke, the dew drops were still fresh on the grass around them. Lilly ran her fingers along the grass and then rubbed them together. "There is something lovely about dew."

"Enjoy it—who knows when or if we will ever see it again," Leon told her grimly as he quickly got up and began packing the horses.

"Why does everyone assume we are going to die going into the desert?" Lilly protested, taking her horse's reins.

"That's just us, Lilly, all doom and gloom." K winked and mounted up.

"With a dash of crazy—don't forget that," Voltaire added, getting on his steed.

"And all driven by obsession," Finnegan sighed, mounting up as well.

Chapter 17

Rune sat at his large dark walnut desk tapping a rolled-up scroll in his hand when he heard the dulcet sound of a bell ringing.

"What is this? Do I have guests?" The mage stood and headed to a large copper bowl filled with pristine water. Taking his cane, he touched the glowing amber globe onto the water ever so gently and watched it ripple, then grow still. There he saw the visage of five "visitors" on their way to see him. One particular visitor caught his eye and his brow rose slightly. "Well, aren't you a handsome one?" He tapped the bowl again and the image disappeared. He set the cane on the floor and leaned on it, his amber- and gold-ringed forefinger tapping against it as he tried to decide what to do. It had been a while since anyone had dared to visit. Then again, those who tried died along the way.

"They need to be found worthy," he decided and headed to the stand where his crow sat preening his feathers. "I need you to send word...my friend." He snapped his fingers and a small scroll appeared. Rolling a string around it, he handed it to the bird, who grabbed the string and took off.

It flew to the campsite where the hired mercenaries were staying and dropped the message to the leader. Unrolling it, he saw the picture of the sword meaning no mercy. The mage had made the message easy for them to understand since none of them could read. Sword meant kill, Raven meant interrogate, and goblet meant allow them to pass. "Come on, boys!" he shouted. "Time to earn our pay!" The men roared in excitement as they headed out.

When the crow returned Rune smiled. "Shall we watch what transpires?" The bird tilted his head. "Yes, let's."

Returning to the copper bowl, he touched it again with his cane and watched the scene unfold.

Voltaire and the others had been loping through the sand for a few hours, slowing as they caught sight of the tower. Voltaire halted and raised his hand to signal to the others to stop. He saw a crow emerge from the tower and fly down to a group of men who were camped just ahead.

"I don't think I like this," Voltaire said as his horse snorted and pawed the sand.

"What do you want to do?" Finnegan asked, riding up beside Voltaire and watching the other men's actions. "They don't seem very welcoming."

"I say we bust some heads," Leon said, shielding his eyes from the bright sun.

"We could say we are coming to join their band," K offered.

"Perhaps, but I don't think— Wait, where did they go?" Voltaire demanded as he looked around.

"The mage is doing something," Leon muttered, looking around.

Lilly's horse, feeling something touch its flank, reared up in panic, sending Lilly flying.

"Lilly!" Leon shouted. He dismounted just as the mercenaries appeared. They tossed the bottles from their hands, the invisibility potion having done its work, and quickly went on the offensive, closing the distance between themselves and the others.

Before Leon could get to Lilly, she was struck hard as she struggled to get up and was then quickly stabbed. In a rage, Leon grabbed the attacker's head and snapped his neck. Voltaire used his sword to block a blow meant for Leon.

"LEON, FOCUS!" Voltaire yelled. Leon turned around and grabbed the mercenary who had tried to kill him, while Voltaire pulled a dagger from his jacket and shoved it into the mercenary's neck. Leon let him drop, then took out his axe as the next man came rushing toward them.

Lilly did her best to focus on her wound to try to at least slow the bleeding, but this one was beyond her ability to heal.

Finnegan's daggers hit their marks as he and K dealt with their own wave of attackers.

"I can't remember the last time we did this together!" Finnegan shouted through the clanging of the blades.

"It has been a while," K grunted as she blocked a blow with her shortsword and slid through the sand, pushed back by the sheer weight of her opponent. Once she had purchase, she kicked her leg out hard and slammed it onto the man's knee. She heard a crack and his scream as he went down. Finnegan spun his sword so it was facing behind him and stabbed the man, saving K from doing it. He knew how much she hated killing with a blade. His other sword sliced the neck of another mercenary approaching him from the front.

"Thanks," K said as they met up and went back to back, readying for the next wave.

Voltaire and Leon took out the last two near them, one with an axe to the head—splitting it almost in half—and the other with a dagger through the throat. They headed toward K and Finnegan. The four grouped up and glanced up at each other with a nod. Having gained the upper hand, they made quick work of the remaining men.

Once the last man dropped, Leon rushed back to Lilly. "LILLY!" He fell to the ground, putting his hand on her wound to keep pressure on it.

"It's okay, I stopped— I stopped the bleeding." She coughed and blood shot out. The others knelt around her, trying to come up with a plan to save her.

Rune watched them for a moment before sighing. "Well, they did kill all my mercenaries...and that redhead looks rather interesting...and I have been bored," he mused. "All right." Rune tapped his cane on the floor and a portal opened. He straightened up his robe and then walked through.

"I assume you are trespassing for a reason." Rune's multicolored eyes scanned the bleeding group as he ran his fingers through his wavy black hair.

Leon was bandaging up Lilly, who had gone unconscious—and was thus unable to heal herself—when the mage appeared. "You bastard! You did this! Heal my sister, you asshole!" He charged at Rune, who smacked Leon on the chest with his cane, sending him flying back and hitting the ground hard.

"That is no way to speak to your would-be savior, and attacking me earns you no favors." Rune looked down at them and a moment later felt a telltale tingling. One of them had magic. He looked at each of them and his eyes finally landed on the young girl. "Come, bring the girl and be on your best behavior. I have little patience." He spun around, his long dark blue cloak flying behind him as he walked through the portal.

"Are you sure about this?" K asked, helping Lilly up. Voltaire was white as a sheet and looked as if he were about to snap.

"We don't have a choice—he is going to heal Lilly or die," Voltaire snarled, following the mage and trailed by Leon, who was carrying Lilly.

"Mages," Finnegan scoffed as he took K's hand and entered the portal as well. K was the last to step through the portal before it closed.

They emerged in a small study. Voltaire was seconds from attacking the mage when Rune turned around and, placing a hand on Lilly's head, healed her instantly. Her eyes fluttered open and she looked up at Leon, who had a look of relief on his face. Then she saw Voltaire, who looked relieved but angry at the same time.

"Tell me, little mage, where did you study?" Rune asked, ignoring everyone else, though he did look up at the strapping lad holding her.

"I didn't learn from anyone. I grew up on the streets with my brother." She glanced up at Leon.

How interesting, Rune thought. "That would explain what happened during that battle. You need training and you're in luck. I'm looking for an apprentice—it will be you." He snapped his fingers and she was suddenly wearing robes of a trainee.

"Hey! What do you think you're doing?!" Voltaire protested and took a step forward, but a sharp glance from the mage stopped him in his tracks. "What twisted game are you playing?"

"Such a thick-headed lot," Rune sighed, then looked over at Finnegan and K. "Well, you two seem a bit more levelheaded. Tell me, what are you here for?"

Lilly was still a bit stunned at suddenly becoming this archmage's apprentice. It was something she had always wanted, but at what price?

"We came looking for a scrying mirror...one that can help summon the dead," K said, folding her arms, her face stoic.

"Ahhh, I know the one of which you speak. And why, pray tell, would you need such a mirror? The only one among you who has any magic is this one, but she would not have the knowledge to use it." His brows lifted in curiosity. His curled black mustache and the small manicured patch of hair on his chin was a bit of a surprise to K. That was high fashion, all the rage—how did he know that out here?

"It's for our employer, Sephtis," Finnegan replied.

"Oh, ho, this is just delicious. Are you talking about *the* Sephtis? One-time noble who saved the King of Chamberre and his family? Once a prolific healer who turned to the dark arts of necromancy, disowned and run out of his town for grave-robbing and other unseemly acts? Please tell me it's that Sephtis." Rune's eyes glittered.

K shifted her weight. This mage sure knew a lot about Sephtis. "Yes, that is the one."

"Hahaha! Is he still trying to resurrect his wife and kids? Crazy bastard." Rune laughed, though the sound was not a friendly one.

"Actually, he's helping me get my wife back," Voltaire sassed back.

Rune gave him a long meaningful stare before saying, "You know, there is a reason it's a forbidden art. The dead should stay dead. Move on."

Voltaire's eyes flashed and he stepped forward, but Lilly grabbed his arm. "Please, we would just like the mirror. What would it take to get it?"

Rune regarded Lilly, then the group. "You become my apprentice and I will allow you to borrow my mirror. But where that mirror goes, I go. Besides, I need to get out some and it would be interesting to finally meet this Sephtis."

"All right, agreed," Lilly said. "At least, to me being your apprentice." She glanced over at K, who nodded at her approvingly.

"All right, mage, we need that mirror, so I guess you are coming with us. But first we need some healing. Lilly wasn't the only one hurt in your little ambush." She smirked, expecting no less. Even Sephtis had some nasty surprises for unwanted visitors. "I had hoped to sneak my way in here, but I should have known better."

"Indeed, you should have." Rune appraised the bedraggled and wounded group. Well, he was the one who had sent the mercenaries on them. He tapped his cane on the ground and a healing wind blew around the room.

Lilly's eyes widened in delight. "That was amazing! How did you... Your cane, is it magical?"

Rune's lips curled into a sly grin and his eyes glittered with excitement. "The cane has some magic. It helps amplify my natural abilities, as well as storing power. We will need to see what works best for you. I have a cane because... Well, that's another story." He turned around and headed toward his crow. "Ready for some traveling?" The bird tilted its head and jumped up on his shoulder.

"Now excuse me for just a moment." He disappeared and then reappeared a few moments later with a bulging pack, his crow perched on his shoulder.

"You must show me that trick." Lilly was practically giddy.

Voltaire's brows drew together. He did not like this arrangement or the way the mage looked at her, but he had no other choice. "Let's go. We need to get back to the horses and head to the docks."

"Well, your horses are on their way back to the stable you bought them from..." Rune was staring into what looked like a pocket compass. "Well, then, I guess we shall just take a portal." He tapped his cane and whispered a few words and the portal opened up. He motioned for everyone to step through.

"Wait," said Leon, his voice laced with incredulity "After all this, we are just going to trust him? He sent his mercenaries on us! He almost got Lilly killed!"

"I don't like it either, but we are alive and we have to get the scrying mirror," Voltaire said, gritting his teeth.

Leon looked over at Finnegan, who shrugged and gently pushed K through the opening. Having worked for a mage and hunted down other mages, Finnegan was not unfamiliar with this kind of scenario. Leon's large fists curled as he glared at Rune. Voltaire gave a wary look but walked through the portal after the couple. Leon wouldn't move, not trusting the mage.

Rune clicked his tongue in irritation. "You are angry, but I have a right to defend myself." Then, flashing an unsettling but charming smile, he added, "But if it makes you feel any better, I was rooting for you."

"Oh, if you were so worried about us killing you, why do you trust us now?" Leon pressed.

"I am a good judge of character." Rune sniffed and tilted his chin up.

Leon's hands were on his hips and he gave Rune a long look as he wrestled with conflicted feelings. "Fine." Turning around, he headed into the portal.

Everyone but Lily had gone through, which left her alone with Rune for a moment. "The large one is your twin brother?" he asked nonchalantly.

"Yes," she said, her voice holding surprise. "Most don't get that."

"Well, I'm not like most, but I'm sure you've gathered that. You are a bright girl, after all." His smile was small, but she caught it and she smiled wide as she headed into the portal.

"Well, Rhys, let's see what trouble we can get into, shall we?" Rune asked the crow and it cawed as they entered the portal.

Chapter 18

When they returned to the docks Voltaire was quick to get his men gathered and ready to leave port. As he stood on deck he saw Lilly grab her things and excitedly chatter at Rune about staying in a cabin with him so she could begin her training right away.

K walked over to Voltaire, hands in her pockets. "You look...irritated." She tilted her head, watching him.

"I don't like this new mage." It was truth—well, *partial* truth.

"Uh-huh. Well, I don't think anyone does except, well... Lilly. But just remember, you need him, unless you've changed your mind..."

Voltaire looked at her sharply. "Why would I change my mind?"

"I don't know. There have been warning signs...and there is the opportunity for a new life, with new friends. We could focus on finding your children." She kept her voice calm as she said this.

"My children need their mother," he retorted.

"They need their father, too," she replied and then held her hands up when his eyes flashed angrily at her. "All right, all right... I'll go check on...something." He turned around and headed down the stairs. Her eyes landed on Finnegan and she smiled at how lucky—and how absolutely terrified—she was. Good things always came with a side of bad. What would that bad be? she wondered.

"We're ready to set sail, Captain!" Finnegan's voice echoed.

"All right, men, you know what to do!" Voltaire called and the men set to work. Before long the galleon was riding the waves, heading back to Sephtis's island.

As the ship rocked gently on the waves Rune was busy working with Lilly on rudimentary skills as a mage. He was impressed with how quickly she was learning and how eager she was.

The door swung open and Leon strode into the room. "You coming to eat?" he asked as he took off his shirt, poured water into the bowl, and proceeded to wash himself.

Rune hid the smile that was begging to break free as he looked the handsome Leon over.

"Who made food?" Lilly asked, her cheeks turning rosy. She was the cook, so if someone else had to cook that meant she was slacking on her duties.

"Haggis did," Leon said flatly. Haggis was not the best of cooks.

"Oh..." Lilly frowned. "I am sorry. I got sidetracked."

"Don't apologize to me," he chuckled. "It's the men who are grumbling. You spoiled them and now they want it all the time. Poor Haggis is doing his best."

"Well, then, perhaps we should stay hidden to avoid the wrath of the sailors." Rune leaned back with a smile on his lips.

Leon shook his head. "They are a crafty bunch. They would just come here and drag you out."

"Well, then, let's just meet this unruly horde head on..." Rune stood and held his arm out to Lilly, who smiled brightly and wrapped her arm around him. "Lead the way, Leon."

Leon grabbed a clean shirt, opened the door, and headed to the galley, where the men were grumbling as they carried their food to their posts.

"Never again!" Haggis thundered, slamming his spoon down. He turned around to Lilly and glared at her. "I see you've finally deigned to grace us with your presence. Did you forget you have a job, lass? This is not some leisure cruise. You are part of the crew and you pull your weight!"

"Haggis..." Leon started to warn him.

"Shut up, you lummox; she's not a child," Haggis shot back and pushed past them.

"Charming bunch they are." Rune stroked Rhys's feathers.

"That's because they are pirates who haven't done any raiding and they are antsy." Leon shrugged. "Eventually we will have to do something about it before they all mutiny."

"Are they not getting paid?" Rune inquired, pleased that Leon had stopped scowling at him, for the moment at least.

"They are, but they want adventure, too. They are pirates. They want pillage and plunder." He stared into the pot and frowned. "I'm gonna skip this."

"Pillaging and plundering, sounds fun..." Rune said as he looked around. "Well, it seems everyone has abandoned dinner."

"I should make something. The crew is probably going to get more irritable and maybe sick looking at that stew." Lilly headed over to the kitchen and started to clean up.

Rune leaned on his cane and smiled at Leon. "Would you be interested in a game?"

Leon turned to look at Rune. He had expected some old ugly mage, hunched over with wrinkles to the floor, but instead Rune was tall and lithe with a wry smile and eyes that always looked a different color and then all colors at once. "Depends on the game," he sniffed. Glancing over at Lilly he saw her humming softly. He smiled—she only hummed when she was happy.

"Chess." Rune snapped his fingers and a board appeared with the pieces ready.

"Ahhh, I should have known." Leon sat down. "All right, mage, a game... Shall we make a bet?"

Rune laughed. "All right, what do you wish to bet?"

"I will owe you a favor if you win, and vice versa." Leon leaned his elbows on the table.

"Hmmm, that would be interesting, all right. White goes first... Let's play." The crow jumped down onto the table and settled by the board. "Don't mind Rhys. He likes to play with the pieces when they come off the board."

Leon smiled at the crow. "As long as he doesn't steal them off the board."

"He may try, but he's a bit obvious about it. Thinks he's being sneaky." Rune spoke fondly of his little friend.

"Well, then, let's play." Leon made the first move.

Rune tapped the rook on the table as he contemplated his move. This Leon was much smarter than he looked. He sighed and rubbed his chin.

"You know there are no more moves left," Leon said, leaning back and chuckling as he watched the mage frown and shoot him a look of disgust. "You might as well accept the inevitable."

"Fine." He tipped his Queen over. "You win." Rune was barely able to hold back his annoyance.

"I heard you were bit of a sore loser." Leon flashed a wicked smile, goading the mage.

Rune's eyes narrowed and he snapped his fingers, setting the board back up into place. "And where, pray tell, did you hear that?"

Leon spun the board around. "I'll let you go first. It was just a story about you and what you did when you didn't make archmage." The tone implied he could have cared less, but Leon was holding back intense curiosity about this mage.

Rune bristled and his lip curled. "They were fools not to choose me. I was obviously the better choice. Nepotism won the day, not skill." Grabbing a pawn, he moved it without really thinking.

"I hear you did something rather spectacular when you quit the mages' guild." Leon made his move, then looked over at Rune, who was watching him with mild curiosity.

"Oh, you weren't told?" Rune asked, making his move with a bit more focus. Rhys was hopping onto the table, looking at the pieces on the board. He was focusing mainly on Leon's side.

"Hey, I see you..." Leon looked at Rhys, reached into his pocket, and pulled out a shiny-looking rock. At first he wanted to give it to Lilly but thought it might keep Rhys occupied. He placed it front of Rhys, who cawed loudly and bounced around it, then picked it up in his mouth and carried it around for a moment before bringing it to Rune. "And no, I wasn't told." He contemplated his move, glancing over at Rune, who focused on his small companion.

"That is quite a lovely stone you have there," Rune told Rhys. "We will add it to your collection. But I'll keep it out so you can admire it for now." He smiled warmly at Rhys and ran his fingers gently over the bird's head. Rhys leaned into the petting and then pushed his stone a bit.

Leon couldn't help but notice the change in Rune whenever it came to Rhys. There was gentleness and a great deal of affection—rather the opposite of his character when it came to humans. He made his move, then motioned to Rune that it was his turn.

"Well, if you must know, I got them all out of their rooms, locked up their doors with a very difficult barrier to dispel, and then made all their clothes disappear. They were all locked out of their rooms, naked, and looking to the new archmage to save them from embarrassment. It took that pompous archmage almost four days to break the spell." Rune made his move.

Leon burst out laughing. "I think I like you, mage." Leon continued laughing as he made his move and Rune did his best to ignore the sudden burst of happiness at the idea.

"What's not to like?" He gave Leon a wry smile.

Leon cleared his throat and stared directly into Rune's eyes. "I think its your move."

"Is it? I thought I already made it." Rune stared back at him and moved his piece. "Checkmate."

For the next few days Rune worked with his new apprentice, getting her started on some basic elemental control. Since they were on a ship, he began teaching her how to help focus the wind into the sails. Leon would watch them when he took the wheel, but he found his gaze would often land longer on Rune than his sister. Their nights were often spent talking and playing chess while Lilly would finish up her duties and then practice what she had learned.

K went into the mess hall where she once again saw Rune and Leon. They were both leaned forward, focused equally on the game and each other. "Oh, this is perfect," K whispered and made her way over. "Rune, seems you spend more time with Leon than you do your own apprentice." She held back the giddiness she felt.

Rune gave her a snarling look. "My apprentice is very adept. I don't need to hold her hand. Isn't there a certain pirate you should be mounting?"

"Isn't there a certain pirate you wish to mount?" K saw Rune begin to stand and she took off running, her laughter echoing.

Rune's frown deepened and he stopped for a moment.

"Don't let K get to you," Leon said soothingly. "She loves stirring things up."

"No, that's not it...something feels off." Rune snapped his fingers and the chessboard disappeared. He got up, paused, picked up the small shiny stone they'd been using to keep Rhys occupied while they'd played, and slipped it into the pocket of his robe before heading to the deck.

Once up top, he looked at the skies. It was clear out and the stars blinked at him, but there was something in the air he couldn't put his finger on. "We should change course," Rune said, looking at Leon.

Finnegan was walking by and overheard Rune. "The skies are fine. The course we are on will get us to Septhis the fastest."

Leon looked over at Rune, who shook his head. "Leon, you should talk to Voltaire. He might listen to you."

"I'll try," said Leon. "See you in the cabin." Leon headed up to the wheel where Voltaire was standing. "Captain, you got a moment?"

Voltaire looked over to see Leon and smiled. "Of course!" He motioned for Leon to come up.

"Rune says we should change course," Leon told him without wavering. "He senses something off."

Voltaire raised a brow and looked out at the sky. "I've been sailing my entire life, Leon. I can't see a storm coming, but I will keep an eye out."

Leon nodded and headed back to the cabin where Rune was talking to Lilly. "Well, I talked to Voltaire, but he seems to think we will be all right."

Rune grumbled something unintelligible but said nothing else.

Leon shrugged and headed to his bunk.

"Can you sense it, Lilly?" Rune asked his apprentice, who closed her eyes and then slowly nodded.

"I can't explain it. But something feels...off," Lilly agreed.

"I fear that feeling will only get worse." Rune sighed, leaning on his cane.

Finnegan boomed, "Captain!! We are on a forced course! We need to abandon ship!" He slid across the deck as the ship began to tip and a rush of water poured over the bow. The storm had come out of nowhere. They were so close to the main island, but they were being steered by the storm to a small island they could barely see. The coastline was nothing but jagged rocks and would tear the ship apart once they reached it. Voltaire tried his best to fight the raging tempest, to no avail. They were heading straight for that jagged coast.

Voltaire cursed as he looked starboard. If they jumped now, they might be able to make it. Looking down, he saw Rune grabbing hold of Lilly when she began falling away from him. "Rune! Don't you have some spell!" He ignored the I-told-you-so glare the mage was giving him.

Rune was soaked. He had warned them, but they had only ignored him. When Rhys had left, his stomach had dropped and moments later the storm had struck. "With this many people, I don't know if it will work, but if you wish it, I will try," he called back.

"Do it!!" Voltaire called as another gush of water almost made him lose his footing. He heard Lilly scream, but he was too focused on keeping the ship steady to see what had prompted her scream.

Finnegan grabbed hold of K, and along with Leon, the two of them headed toward Rune. They had to make sure he could focus while casting his spell, so they did their best to keep him safe.

Rune spoke his words, doing his best to concentrate, the amber on his cane warming until it started to glow and almost seemed on fire. When he slammed his cane onto the deck there was an explosion of light and then complete darkness for everyone.

When Rune's eyes started to slide open he looked around. They had arrived on dry land. Leon was near him and he saw K along with a few men sprawled across the beach. But he did not see Voltaire or Finnegan. Rolling up, he groaned slightly when he saw Rhys flying and landing on a piece of driftwood. "I see you made it," he grumbled, trying to get up, but his cane was lying far away from him. "Damn it."

Leon got up and shook his head, sand falling everywhere. He saw Rune's cane and grabbed it. Heading over to him, he leaned down, grabbed his arm, and pulled him up.

"Where's Finnegan! Where's Voltaire!" K said as she shot up out of the sand and began running around.

Lilly was still unconscious.

"What did you do, mage!!" K screamed and rushed toward Rune.

Before she could reach him, Leon stopped her, wrapping his arms around her waist. "Stop it!" he demanded. "Calm down!"

K instantly regained her composure.

"I'm sorry." She relaxed and went to Lilly. "I think something hit her head."

"Let me see." Rune, with Leon's help, went to his apprentice. Leaning down, he touched her forehead and her eyes fluttered open. "There we go!"

Everyone stood up and looked around. The men had begun to wake and come over to them.

"Well, it seems the spell sent us all here... But most likely all over this island," Rune mused. "All right, then, we will go look for them." He turned to the men. "Listen up. Start making a camp here! Gather food, water, and supplies. Salvage what has washed ashore." He glanced into the sea and saw the *Wicked Damsel* crashed upon rocks. "If anyone wishes to brave the sea to the *Wicked Damsel* for supplies, feel free to do so."

"I don't want to leave the girls here alone," Leon muttered. "They need to come with us."

"Yes, I don't think that would be wise." Rune had already caught many lecherous gazes at the women. "Can you walk, Lilly?"

The young girl nodded. "I can. We need to find them." The young mage was worried about Voltaire. Was he all right? Was he hurt? Pulling up her dress, she began walking determinedly down the beach.

"Wait! Hold on! Wait for me!" K ran after her.

Leon looked over at Rune. "How is your leg?" Rune had never given an explanation for his slight limp and use of a cane, but Leon could tell at times it bothered him.

Rune's eyes flashed as he looked over at Leon. "It's fine for now."

"You are rather touchy about your leg." His lip flickered as he took pleasure in poking the mage.

"I have reason to be," Rune snapped. Walking in the sand was hard work. He spent more time focusing on walking than he did looking for the others.

"Well, I can always carry you if you get too tired," Leon offered.

At any other time he would have taken that invitation to flirt with him, but on this occasion he was too tired.

Leon looked over at Rune. He seemed a bit off, but Leon refrained from saying so, just keeping his eyes out for anything suspicious as the girls called out for Voltaire and Finnegan. It was getting late and they still had found no sign of the captain and his first mate, though they did find other sailors, whom they guided back toward the rest of the group.

Lilly was pacing the ground. "Wait..." she slapped her hand on her forehead. "You have the scrying mirror! Can't we look for them that way? Or does it only work for the dead?"

Despite his exhaustion, Rune smiled. "That is...an excellent idea, and no it doesn't just work for the dead." He pulled out the small pocket-sized mirror from around his neck. "Do you have something of Finnegan's or Voltaire's?"

K walked over to him and handed him a bracelet made of twine. It was a silly piece that he had made one night for her on the ship, but she didn't ever take it off.

"Perfect." He opened the mirror, placed the bracelet around it, and began reciting the incantation in a soft, low tone. Moving the bracelet aside, in the mirror he saw an image of the two men on the rocky part of the beach. They were unconscious but breathing.

"Where, though, are they...on this island?" Lilly asked, looking into the mirror. Leon looked into it as well and sighed. "They are on the eastern side...all these islands are similar. The western sides are full of sandy beaches while the eastern sides are rocky... We should have gone the other way." He glanced behind him.

"Can't we just cut through the woods?" K asked, feeling frustrated.

"Not now, it's dangerous," Leon told her, seeing her edge closer to the woods.

"Something...isn't right." Rune hesitated and began glancing around. Rhys fluttered his wings unhappily. "What do either of you know about these islands?" Rune looked at Leon and Lilly.

"Just their topographical layout... Most of the islands, save a few, have farmlands where they grew grapes for winemaking." he shrugged when Lilly's eyes widened and she glanced around nervously. "What is it, Lilly?"

"There is a story about one of these islands..." Her voice sounded nervous.

"What story is that?" Leon coaxed.

"There was a landowner who had purchased one of the islands. When he arrived he was surprised to find a small colony of fey living there. But instead of working with them he chose to try to destroy them, so he brought in mages of all kinds and they slaughtered the fey. Before the last fey was killed, she cursed them all, that any who touched this land would meet their deaths one way or another. Eventually they all did. One by one they died horrific deaths. Some said it was the island, some said it was the spirits, but no one knows. But the landowner refused to give up and brought more people across, even his wife and children... Before the month was even up, they all died. He was left all alone... No way to get off the island. It is said he went mad and eventually died. No one dared to go on the island after that, even the King and Queen forbade it."

K stared at Lilly. "And you think we are on that island now?" K was trying to stay calm.

Lilly nodded. "I do."

"Fantastic." K threw up her hands.

"Easy now," said Rune. Let's not get ahead of ourselves. Let's get some rest and we will start heading back. Early in the morning." But even Rune felt the hairs on the back of his neck standing on end. He had felt something sinister the moment he had woken.

Leon was able to gather enough driftwood and Lilly lit the fire. The girls scooted closer and lay down, both falling asleep from exhaustion. Leon sat down with Rune. "How bad is it?" He kept his voice low so the girls wouldn't wake.

"There is a darkness here...intent on killing trespassers," Rune said. "We must be respectful to them. In the morning we will gather supplies and try and do a peace offering." As he said this, he adjusted himself and rubbed his thigh.

"You know you are terrible at that... Here, let me." Leon cracked his fingers. "Where exactly does it hurt?"

Rune looked at Leon for a moment, a small smile appearing on his face for the first time in days. "Right here." He pointed to his upper-thigh hip area.

"All right, let me see here." Leon placed his hands on the mage and began working his fingers into the muscles.

Rune winced at first but then moaned as the aching tension began to go away. "And here I thought you were making things up for a chance to touch me."

Leon chuckled and kept working. "You must be feeling better—your quick tongue is back."

"Or maybe it's your ministrations bringing it out in me," Rune sighed, stretching back. "Thank you, Leon," he said, his relief evident. For the first time the pain actually went away. "Your fingers are better than magic."

Leon chuckled. "You think so?"

Rune's eyes flashed for a moment and he just gave a dark smile and settled back down, wrapping his cloak around him.

"I'll leave you to your dirty thoughts about me," Leon teased and lay back, closing his eyes.

"As will I. I know that look too well," Rune replied, smirking and closing his eyes.

Rune woke up feeling better. Even though he could feel the pain slowly making its way back, his leg still felt a thousand times better than it had before. For a moment his insides quivered as he thought about last night and then he growled inwardly. No, he was going to be strong. Leon would bow to his will! No man had ever gotten the better of him, and by the gods it wasn't going to happen now!

"Good, you're awake," K said in relief. Leon had told her not to wake Lilly or Rune since mages needed their rest.

"Yes. I see you are ready to go," Rune murmured, still dealing with an internal battle.

The small group began making their way back toward where they had left the sailors, but to their horror the men were already dead, torn to shreds. Limbs were scattered across the beach, the sand soaked in blood.

Lilly's stomach lurched and K went pale. "What...what is this?" K gasped, looking around.

"It's the forest...this island..." Lilly's voice rose an octave.

"Easy, Lilly." Leon wrapped his arm around her. "I thought all the Fey had gone. Didn't they all disappear after the plague? They were hit the hardest."

"Maybe they just came to these islands." K shrugged, trying to keep her calm.

"Or... Maybe they are on the other side of the barrier in Gareen," Lilly offered. "The plague came from them, but there was no plague there—they made sure of that."

"That is plausible." Rune scanned the horizon. "There seem to be a few men out in the water." Rune motioned with his cane and everyone turned to look.

Heading over to them, Leon recognized Haggis right away "Haggis! You old bastard, you survived. Too salty for even the sea, aye?" Leon clapped the older pirate's shoulders.

Haggis grunted, "See you made it nice and easy. We landed in the water and when we went to the wood to get some firewood, the blackest of tendrils exploded from the ground and began ripping the lads limb from limb. We only survived because we ran back into the water and those limbs stopped chasing."

He grunted and looked up at the lad. "Have you seen the captain?" Haggis rubbed his hands together and sighed, looking off into the sea that was now calm. Bright blue skies were up above and soft white sand beneath their feet. It looked like paradise as long as one didn't examine too closely or wander off shore.

Leon was about to answer him when K yelled in panic.

"We have to find Finnegan and we have to find him NOW!" Her eyes flashed to Rune, who was already looking at the scrying mirror.

"They are not where they were yesterday," Rune sighed. "They are in the heart of this island." Rune tried not to roll his eyes. He knew K was going to demand they head into the forest. But instead of asking, K just turned around and began marching straight into the woods.

"K! Wait!" Lilly rushed after her. "You can't just go in there! It's dangerous! Please, let's come up with a plan!" Finally reaching K, she grabbed her arm firmly. "I want in there just as badly as you do, but it will do no good to go in half-cocked!"

K spun around, frustrated and ready to lash out, but seeing Lilly's gentle face, she bit her lip and held back. "Do you have any type of plan?"

Lilly's brow furrowed for a moment as she thought and then her face lit up. "It seems as if the island only attacks those who attack it. We need to make sure we do nothing that seems like an aggressive action toward the woods. No fires, no cutting. When we walk, we make sure we don't even snap a twig! I can try to connect with the forest itself like I did with the Twisted Forest."

"Oh, dear gods, we are going to get attacked by this island for accidentally stepping on a bug," Leon groused. "Haggis, you and these men stay at the edge of the land. Only use what you've salvaged. Don't go any farther in!"

Haggis nodded and he and the other two men who had survived moved to the edge, but did not move any closer in.

Leon rubbed his brow. "You really ready to do this?" He looked at K and Lilly.

The girls nodded and Leon glanced back at Rune. "And you?"

Rune gave him a wry smile. "It will be fun."

They all moved closer together, took in a deep unified breath, and let it go. Lilly, taking the lead, walked right into the forest, trying to connect to it. It seemed to be working as they carefully plotted their way around tree limbs, roots, and shrubs, trying their best not to disturb anything. Rune held onto the scrying mirror and watched to see if they were getting any closer.

"Move a bit more left," he whispered and nodded to himself.

Shifting, they followed Lilly's footsteps and Rune's guidance. The sun was starting to lower and panic began to set in for K. They had not found Finnegan or Voltaire...and it would be dark soon.

"We should split up!" K shouted. "Cover more ground!" She stepped away from the others as they paused to get their bearings again.

"It's not safe that way, K!" Leon reminded her. "You know that."

K let out a frustrated growl and threw her hands up. Pacing away from the others, she tripped over a root covered by a bush and threw her hands out to catch herself. Her fingers wrapped around a small branch, but with her momentum she pulled it right off of the tree. Not even realizing what she had done, she stood up angrily, tossed the branch away, and found three sets of eyes gazing at her.

"What?" She looked at them and then it dawned on her. "Oh, shit." The ground opened up and with a terrified scream K fell into the deep chasm.

"K!!" Lilly took off after her, and in her haste fell in after K.

Leon had run over to try to catch Lilly but was a mere moment too late. Falling to his knees, he tried to dig his way through the dirt to get to her. Fluette could not be dead. No! It was not possible!

His nails were bleeding and Rune put his hand on Leon's shoulder. "Leon..." He sent calming energy through his body. "Leon, stop...you need to stop." He grabbed the warrior's hands.

Leon gripped the mage's hand tight. "I have to find her... I can't..."

"We will find her, but not this way," he promised, wincing slightly at how hard Leon was gripping him, but not objecting.

"We have too," Leon murmured.

Chapter 19

Voltaire groaned and touched his head. Blood was dripping from it. "Where the hell..." he griped, trying to sit up. He was in some sort of pit. Finnegan was next to him and not moving. Voltaire rushed over to Finnegan and shook him. "Hey... Finn!"

There was no response.

"Damn it." Voltaire checked his pulse—it was faint but there. He began looking for wounds. His head was pounding, but it was more important to figure out what was wrong with Finnegan. He found a blood-drenched wound on his thigh and frowned. This wasn't good. How much blood had he lost?

He took off his jacket, tore off his tunic, and began tearing it into strips and tying these around the pirate's leg. Once he felt the tourniquet was tight enough, he stood up.

"Hello? Is there anyone out there?" Voltaire called, his voice frustrated and trying to hold back panic.

Something stirred in the air and a woman appeared covered in roots. "You are trespassing, human. You have not harmed us...yet."

Voltaire, sensing danger, relaxed and bowed in respect. "Forgive me. My friends and I were traveling to a different island when the storm had us crashing upon your shores. We do not mean any harm."

"Is that so?" Her disembodied voice floated through the air, her breath creating mist. "Then why did your men begin tearing down my forest! Polluting her with their filth!" Her once-equanimous tone turned angry.

"They did not know this was your island, my lady. They were looking for shelter and a way to leave this place," he guessed. "Just as am I and my friend here." He pointed down.

The woman seemed to float slightly in front of them, the tendrils of her body curling and unfurling around her. Voltaire saw her whole body start to shudder as her hand reached up, feeling something or someone moving above. Her white eyes lifted and the ground violently split apart, causing two figures to plummet into the gaping pit and slam down hard onto its bottom surface.

"What of these two? Are they your friends who mean no harm?" she hissed.

"Yes...yes, they are." He bent down, grabbed K, pulled her up, and whispered, "Don't do anything stupid." He trusted she wouldn't, as she tended to be levelheaded—except when it came to Finnegan, in which case she lost all common sense and rationality. "Go help him." He moved her over to Finnegan and K paled and rushed over to him.

Lilly stood and stared in awe at the creature before him. "It is *you*! You, you are *alive*!" she beamed, prompting the creature to look at her with surprise.

"You sound...happy for me." The shock was evident in her voice.

"I am! I am! Did only you survive? Are there more of your people? Oh, this is wonderful news!"

Voltaire couldn't help but smile. Lilly was always so sweet and genuine.

"There are more of us, yes. After Basile attempted to kill us, we went underground. He thought us dead. He was mistaken." The dirt seemed to whirl around her, sensing the change in mood.

Lilly said sincerely, "Yes, as were many people. I am sorry my friends and I disturbed your peace here. There was a horrible crash. I know the men made a terrible mistake by hurting your woods. But I assure you, my friends here...the two wandering above and the ones on the beach—we do not wish you any harm. All we wish to do is head back home. You have my word."

The wood nymph reached out and vines wrapped around Lilly, who did her best to stay calm. The vines tightened slightly around her, but she felt a warm, gentle probing. When the nymph seemed satisfied, the vines pulled back.

"You speak the truth, Lilly." For a moment the creature smiled, and with a wave of her vine hand, they were above ground. "Head back to your men. There will be a raft waiting for you to take yourself and your men from these shores."

"I promise I will do my best to ward off visitors. This place has already been forbidden, but I will do my best to discourage more people from coming. " Lilly bowed her head and the creature nodded.

Voltaire grabbed Finnegan and threw him over his shoulder. As they headed to the beach, they stumbled into Leon and Rune.

"What in the hell's happened?" Leon exclaimed as he rushed over to them.

"Keep calm and let's keep on walking," Lilly said, grabbing K's arm and pulling her along. "Rune, please look over Finnegan while we walk."

The mage nodded. When he reached Finnegan, he put his hand on his back and began murmuring a healing spell.

Once their feet hit sand, K spotted the men and a raft made of wood and vines that even boasted a large sail.

Haggis, the crusty old pirate, wasted no time getting the men to pull the raft onto the water. Everyone piled onto it and Lilly began focusing her magic to create a wind while the others started paddling.

K was pale. Grabbing hold of Finnegan's hand, she pressed it to her lips and began whispering over and over, "Please don't die...please don't die."

Rune spent all of his magic fixing the wound but Finnegan had lost a lot of blood. "I've done what I can... All we can do now is pray he has the strength to survive until I can recover." Slumping down, he found himself caught in Leon's arms. His smile was brief before he blacked out.

"Is he all right?" Voltaire asked.

"He's used every last bit of his magic to heal Finnegan; his wound was extensive. He will sleep as long as he needs to replenish. It might take a few days." Leon shifted so that Rune was leaning against his chest.

Voltaire nodded. "How are you, Lilly?" He turned to look concernedly at her as she shuddered slightly, doing her best to keep focus.

"I am getting tired... I don't know how much longer I can do this," she replied.

"Take a rest," Voltaire urged, reaching up and taking her hand. She had been standing and holding onto the mast with one arm raised, trying to help guide the raft. "The men can paddle for a while. Can't you, men?"

"Aye, Captain, let the lass rest." Haggis nudged the other men and they grabbed their paddles.

Moments later they heard the cry of a crow. The crow appeared and flew down to land on Leon's shoulder. "So you made it," he murmured, reaching up and stroking the bird's chest. It cawed and cocked its head as it looked down at Rune. "He's just resting. He's fine." The black bird ruffled its feathers, crawled down onto Rune's chest, and settled in.

K was monitoring Finnegan's leg wound. Her hands never left his body, touching him, caressing him. Her words encouraging him to stay with her.

After a few hours the men began to tire of paddling.

Lilly woke, no longer feeling the wind or the raft moving. "My turn again?"

"Are you sure you are doing all right?" Voltaire asked. Leon glanced over, but he said nothing, his fingers running through Rune's hair.

"I will be fine." She touched the mast, closed her eyes, and began casting her spell for the wind.

"I think I see something!" Haggis called, looking out. "I think it's a ship!"

"Lilly, can you send us to them?" Voltaire asked.

"Of course I can!" Excited at the prospect of being saved, she used as much power as she could muster to push the small raft.

"It's the *Lyla*!" Haggis shouted and everyone let out a sigh of relief.

As the massive ship drew closer they could see ropes being thrown down. Once the raft was side by side with the galleon, the latter's crew hoisted it up and helped its passengers aboard the larger vessel.

"Sephtis! Sephtis, you have to help! It's Finnegan!" K was rushing to the old man whose eyes, at first angry, suddenly filled with worry. K was never this emotional and it disturbed him. He rushed over to the lad and quickly scanned him over. "The wound on his thigh…it is…magical," he said in surprise.

"Can you heal him? Rune did all he could, but you can do something, can't you?!" K was trembling as she clung to Finnegan.

"Easy, child," Septhis soothed K. "Voltaire, help me get him to my chambers." Reaching out, he touched K's forehead to see if anything was wrong with her, then paused. *My, my, those two have been busy*, he thought. "You need your rest as well. Come."

Sephtis called to the lad at the helm to begin sailing back home. Leon carried Rune to a bed, followed by Lilly, both of them exhausted and ready for some sleep.

Once Finnegan was on the bed, Sephtis looked the boy over. This wound wasn't good. He asked K what had happened, and when she was done, he shook his head. "This Rune did everything I would have done. The best I can do now is try to give him strength. We can only see what will happen."

It tore at him. Finnegan was the same age his son would have been had he survived. Now, here he was dying and there was nothing Sephtis could do…again. But he would not tell little K that… No. She was with child, and as much as he may have been hard on her, Sephtis cared for her just as he did Finnegan, whom he saw as a son. When he had embarked on this path all had abandoned him. Everyone had marked him as mad and evil, but still these two had stayed, even if they'd had their own reasons for doing so. But for a few years they had been a family…a strange one, but a family no less.

Sephtis stayed in the captain's quarters with Finnegan and K while Rune and Lilly took turns focusing the winds on the sails in an effort to quicken their pace. When they docked, there was no waiting. Everyone worked together to get Finnegan into the mansion. The noble pirate had not awoken yet. His brow was covered in sweat and his heartbeat was low. The veins around the wound on his leg were standing out and had begun to turn green. K stuck close, talking to Finnegan the entire time, and Lilly stuck by her to support her as best she could. Leon, Rune, and Voltaire were carrying him and moving as quickly as they could through the treacherous sand, grass clumps, and vines.

"Easy, boys," Sephtis cautioned as the group entered, the servants having already opened the doors for them. "Get him into his room. Then, Lilly, I will need you to watch him while I see if any of my old books contain information about fey magic," The men carried Finnegan to his bed.

"I am going to head back to make sure the ship is secured. Leon?" Voltaire looked over at the other man.

"With you, Captain." Leon gave a curt nod and followed Voltaire out the door.

"I will help Sephtis look through his library. Two sets of eyes are better than one." Rune looked over at Sephtis. "It will give me time to get to know the famous Archmage of Chamberre."

Sephtis said nothing, just motioned for Rune to follow him.

Lilly and K set to removing Finnegan's clothes while servants came and brought bowls of water and towels. K was shaking as she worked, and Lilly grabbed her hands, sending a warm soothing energy into her.

"Take a breath," Lilly said reassuringly. "You can do this."

K took in a shaky breath and nodded. "Okay... Okay."

Downstairs Rune was looking through various books. As he pulled them out and scanned them, he also kept an eye on the crystal coffin holding what he assumed was Voltaire's wife. "You really *do* plan on bringing back the dead."

"What gave it away?" Sephtis asked, grabbing another book.

"I think it was the giant coffin with the lady inside." Rune snickered.

"So you seem to have an opinion." Sephtis's fingers traced down the words.

"Honestly?" Rune rifled through a few pages. "The dead should stay dead, but I have to admit a morbid curiosity as to how you will do it and if it will actually work."

"I spent decades on research—it will work," Sephtis said, slamming the book shut and sighing in frustration.

When the two mages began to tire of scouring Sephtis's books, they decided to take a break and check on Finnegan. They found K sleeping next to him and Lilly passed out on the chair.

"There is nothing more you can do here, Rune," Sephtis said. "Go get your rest. I may need your assistance tomorrow." Sephtis walked over to Finnegan and placed his hand gently on his forehead before gently running his fingers through his hair. Rune could not hear the words Sephtis was saying, but he could feel the protective aura coming from the old mage.

Rune headed down the hall and found an empty room. Setting his things down, he sighed, walked over to the window, and opened it up for Rhys. The large raven fluttered to the edge of the window and dropped down onto one of the tufted chairs. Undressing, he almost groaned getting into the luxurious bed. It was even better than the one he owned. His thoughts briefly flickered to Leon and a small smile tugged his lips before he fell asleep.

Leon and Voltaire returned to the mansion after everything was settled and decided to sit down and have a drink. They sat at the table where they had all played cards earlier and drank their beers in silence. "Do you think he's going to be okay?" Leon asked quietly.

"He's got Septhis, Rune, and Lilly. I think his chances are pretty good," Voltaire replied, draining his beer. "I'm heading to bed."

Leon watched Voltaire get up and walk toward the stairs. Grabbing another beer, he drank it down quickly and then headed to his room. Opening the door, he sighed and began kicking off his boots and pulling off his shirt. The cold breeze had him looking at the open window. As he went over to shut it, he noticed clothes on the floor. Then a ruffle of feathers had him raise his brow.

"What the..." Leon looked around and then noticed a figure on his bed. "Oh." Walking over, he saw the sleeping visage of Rune. For a moment he thought of going to another room, but he was just too tired and he liked the idea of unsettling the mage in the morning. Moving to the other side of the bed, he crawled in, making sure to give the mage his space before he fell asleep instantly.

Chapter 20

Rune's eyes slid open and he rolled over to find himself face to face with Leon. Sitting up abruptly in surprise, he looked around the room feeling a bit confused. *Cheeky bastard,* Rune mused as he looked over at Leon, who was sleeping soundly next to him. His eyes raked the naked back of this man he hoped would soon be his lover. His wide, muscled shoulders made Rune's lip curl in delight. With a wicked grin, he slid over to Leon and grabbed hold of a firm buttock. Leon jerked up in surprise.

"Morning." Rune smirked, squeezing Leon's ass and then sliding out of bed. "As much as I'd like to ravish you, at this moment I have a mage to speak to and a patient to look over." Rune pulled on his robes, chuckling at the sleepy-eyed Leon who was rubbing his eyes with the palms of his hands.

Leon growled, grabbed Rune's robe, and pulled him down for a hard, passionate kiss. When their lips parted they were both gasping. "Good morning. I will see you when you're done talking to Sephtis." His baritone laugh filled the room. For their first kiss it was rather breathtaking. Leon had thought about waiting for a romantic moment, but the moment seemed right now, and he relished unsettling the cocky mage.

"You sly devil..." Rune growled. "You are such a tease." On his way to the door he looked back with a wicked smile. "Don't bother getting dressed."

Leaving the room, he started down the stairs and then spotted Voltaire. "Ah, good captain, perhaps you can tell me where the venerable Sephtis is?"

"Sure." Voltaire led Rune to the laboratory and knocked on the door. "Sephtis, Rune is here."

"Both of you, come in. We need to speak." Sephtis's voice was grave.

Voltaire opened the door and made his way inside, followed by Rune, who spotted the woman encased in crystal and once again couldn't help but raise his brow in fascination.

"Thank you for what you did for Finnegan and for the scrying mirror." Sephtis motioned for them to sit. There were glasses and drinks waiting for them.

"How is Finnegan?" Rune asked, then saw the deep frown on the old man's face.

"He is not good...and that...that is why I need to speak to you." He turned to Voltaire. "My friend... I may need you to make a choice...a difficult one."

"What are you talking about?" Voltaire looked at him confused.

"I... I am not sure Finnegan will survive. If he dies, it will kill K...and she is carrying his child. It may not come to that. But I need you to consider this as you get the final piece. If Finnegan dies...would you allow me to use the spell to bring him back?" Sephtis rubbed his face. "I promised you I would help you to bring your wife back, and if you choose that I will honor your decision. I just ask you to think on it."

Voltaire was stunned to have to choose between his wife—the mother of his children—or a man whom his rescuer loved. "But it may not come to that." He looked at Sephtis, who nodded.

"It may not...but I needed to tell you. Now, are you two ready to go find the third and final piece?" Sephtis ran his fingers through his white hair.

"Indeed. This should be fun." Rune replied with a grin and looked the old man over. "Afterward you and I are going to have a long chat, Sephtis."

"As you wish. The last piece is a crystal ball from the seeress Clovia. She lives in the marshes deep within the old world." Shrugging his shoulders, he held a rolled-up map.

"Then we leave tomorrow," Voltaire said as he took the map from Sephtis.

Thanks to the magical abilities of Rune and Lilly, they were able to travel what would have otherwise been a month-long trip in just a few days. The two mages were exhausted when they finally made port. They still had a ways to go, but everyone was too worried about Finnegan to voice their complaints. They had been told that once they passed the boundaries of the city they would be in the seer's territory. It was up to her whether they would be allowed upon her lands...and whether they would survive.

Upon reaching the marshes they realized they would need a boat to get through and began searching for a way to cross. The trees created a dark canopy that blocked out the sun. The shade was nice during the day, but the darker it got above, the harder it became to see below.

Lilly created a few balls of light to help them as they traveled.

"By the hells, have we been walking in circles?" Leon groused, his hands on his waist as he looked around.

"I think we might have been," Rune agreed.

"Wait, I see something!" Lilly called, pointing over to a small wooden dock and what looked like a boat.

The men turned their heads and looked. "Let's go take a look," Voltaire said, taking the lead.

As they reached the dock they saw a small boat, but inside sat a figure covered in rags. A cackling laugh startled them. "I've been watching you...watching you go in circles and circles."

"Can you help us?" Lilly asked, stepping closer. "We need to find the seer."

"I might help...for a price..." A withered, bony hand reached out. "Give me your hand, young girl."

Lilly went to reach out her hand and Voltaire snatched it back away. "Why? What do you want from her?"

The voice cackled again. "The feel of young skin is...quite lovely."

"Touch mine, then," Leon growled. "We are the same age."

The figure's shoulders seemed to shudder in laughter. "Come aboard. Let us see if we can take you to where you wish to go."

Despite the desperate need to find the seer, there was distinct mistrust in the air as the four carefully made their way onto the boat.

"I suspect you are wishing to see the seeress. None truly travel farther than the city otherwise...except for a bit of adventure." The cloaked figure shoved off.

"Are you the seeress?" Voltaire asked blatantly.

"Ha ha, wouldn't that be easy! But no, I am but a simple servant." The ship moved slowly along the water.

Rune's crow landed back on his master's shoulder, having finished surveying their surroundings in search of clues to the seeress's whereabouts. Stroking his chest, Rune was able to see everything his bird had seen and he nodded.

"See anything?" Leon asked as Rune pet the bird's head.

"Nothing that will help us," Rune sighed.

The hooded man chuckled. "Smart move with the bird. Clovia does love crows."

Rune's hand suddenly went to Rhys, worried the seeress might ask for his friend.

"I think... I think I just saw something roll under the water," Lilly whispered nervously, moving tighter into Voltaire.

"Oh, don't mind the beasties..." Castor lisped. "They like to accompany me. Do not put your appendages in the water lest you wish to have them removed."

Soon they began getting deeper into the marsh and there was no solid ground anywhere. But in the distance lights could be seen.

"This is going by a lot easier than I expected," Leon murmured, looking around.

"That's because she knew you were coming and she was...curious." The hooded figure shifted the boat, sending it toward the lights.

"I'm not sure if that is good news or not," Leon replied dryly.

The boat floated lazily along while under the water's murky depths a flash of light and a roll of scales could be seen. "Bring them to me, Castor."

"I am, my mistress." The boat began to move faster.

The four of them looked up and saw that the trail of lights led to a small shack. The small boat picked up speed and they suddenly found themselves at the floating porch. As their gazes went up the stairway, the door swung open, revealing an old woman. Her white hair, braided and adorned with crystal beads and carved bone, cascaded down her back as she leaned against the doorway.

"Well, well, look what Bones drug in." Her accent was indiscernible.

"Mistress, I brought them as you wished." The hooded figure bowed and moved the ship so that it was lined up with the deck that wrapped around the whole house.

The woman nodded. "You must be Rune..." She pointed, her arm covered with bone charms. "Leon, Lilly, and Voltaire... Come... I have been waiting for you." She motioned for them to follow her inside.

As they began stepping slowly out of the boat, the group cast unsure glances among one another. They had no idea what they were about to step into, but they followed the mysterious lady and went inside. The walls were lined with jars filled with everything from glowing beetles to entrails. Lilly was positive she spotted a fetus of some sort, but refused to keep looking, clinging to Voltaire's arm.

In the center of the room sat a large circular table with a lovely intricate tablecloth and a crystal ball on a golden stand. With a start, Lily realized that the candles on the side tables were perched on human and animal skulls.

"Come now, have a seat." She motioned, sitting down as well.

They all sat down and Voltaire held Lilly's hand in an attempt to still her nervous shaking.

"There is no need to be afraid, child. I will not hurt you." Clovia smiled reassuringly.

"I am— I am sorry," Lilly stuttered. "I do not mean to presume."

"'Tis all right. Now I know why you've come. You wish that which sits before you." Seeress motioned her head.

"It's for a powerful spell..." Rune began explaining, but stopped when the seeress held up her hand.

"Oh, I know what spell it is. But you must know there is a dire price for what it is you wish to do." She looked at all of them forebodingly and her eyes landed on Voltaire. "You should know this spell will only work once. So make your choice wisely."

Voltaire and Rune looked at each other uneasily for a moment. "Does this mean you will give us the ball?" Voltaire asked slowly.

"On one condition... The crow stays with me. Then, when you return with my globe, you may have your friend back." She tapped the table and an elegant cage appeared around Rhys.

Rune growled, "Why?! Why *Rhys.*"

"Tsk, tsk. Because it is the most important thing you have, mage... Well, non-human." She chuckled. "Do not worry. Your crow will be well taken care of...as long as the ball is as well. Do we have a deal?"

Rune paled considerably and his hands clenched tightly. His demeanor darkened and his brow furrowed. He wanted to say no deal and leave, but then he looked at Voltaire and relented through clenched teeth. "We have a deal." Leon stroked Rune's hand and smiled.

Voltaire stood and reached out for the ball. "No!" shouted the seeress "Only a woman may touch the crystal!" Voltaire's hands jerked back and he looked at Lilly.

With a nod Lilly reached out and picked the ball up and Clovia handed her a bag. "If male hands touch the crystal, all magic will be rendered useless." she warned.

"It will only stay in my hands," Lilly vowed, wrapping the ball up and holding it close to her.

"Well, then... T'was a pleasure. I am sure to see you soon." The seeress smiled and the door opened. "Castor will take you back." The seeress gave Lilly a long look. *Perhaps she will be the one to finally bring an end to Gareen's troubles...if she's strong enough.*

They scrambled out, eager to leave this strange home. The trip back was silent. Rune already missed Rhys, and Leon did his best to comfort him.

The trip was blissfully uneventful. As they pulled into the dock, the crew began working to secure the ship. They bustled around the deck while the Voltaire and the others waited impatiently for the plank to be dropped. Once it did, the group quickly made its way toward the main house.

Sephtis stood outside. His eyes were red and he looked exhausted.

"Sephtis, what is wrong?" Lilly asked, rushing to him.

"Finnegan...he died this morning." Sephtis sighed. It was then they could hear the heart-wrenching sobs from K echoing through the house.

"Oh, no!" Lilly rushed past Sephtis to find K.

Leon frowned and looked at Rune. "Come, leave these two to talk." Rune took Leon's hand and headed inside.

Voltaire stood in stunned silence, staring at Sephtis.

"Bring me to the laboratory." His voice was hoarse.

Sephtis brought him down the stairs, where the sobs were even louder, and they tore into Voltaire as he followed the mage down into his laboratory. There, next to his wife, lay the body of Finnegan.

"I never told you my past..." Sephtis walked over to Finnegan and ran his fingers through his hair. "I was part of a noble family, second in power to the King and Queen. I fell in love with Layla when I was fifteen, married her when I was eighteen. Eight years and four beautiful children later we were a happy family. Three girls and one boy..." He stroked Finnegan's hair again. "A plague swept through our town and I worked day and night trying to keep the King and Queen alive along with their children. I tried to save my family as well, but it only seemed to get worse... Eventually my wife and children became sick and I did everything within my power to heal them, to save them. But it was not enough. I was rewarded with more riches and gold than anyone could imagine for saving the royal family and for having lost mine."

He turned to look at Voltaire with anguished eyes. "But I lost them! All of them! First it was my wife, then my youngest daughter, then the twins, and finally...finally, my son. I swore I would find a way to bring them back...or at least know how to help someone else, and in my obsession to bring myself peace I have paid yet another price. I have lost my second son."

Sephtis paused, looked up at Finnegan, and took his hand. He had lovingly cleaned and prepared his body for the ritual in hopes Voltaire might show him grace. "Now I have that power, but the choice is yours, Voltaire. I will understand completely should you choose your wife. But you must choose soon so that we may show proper respect to the body that will be buried."

Voltaire looked at Finnegan and then walked over to Penelope. He had hoped he wouldn't have to make this choice. But as much as he longed to repent to his wife, to his children, he could not bear to see K in such anguish, or lose a companion he also held dear. The guilt he already bore for his failure with his family would be a burden he would willingly suffer to save Finnegan.

Looking down at her, he sighed. "My dearest... I started this journey to bring you back...but along the way I met this crazy girl in love with a just-as-crazy guy... Part of me feels like a complete bastard...but K is just starting out... Finnegan as well. You did not deserve to die...but neither did Finnegan...he died helping me. I owe it to him and I know...I know you would want me to make the right choice. I hope you can forgive me, Penelope." He sighed and stepped back from the crystal coffin, his forehead creased and his eyes moist.

"Save Finnegan, Sephtis. Bring him back for K." Voltaire patted the mage's back. The old man seemed relieved.

"Bring me the crystal ball and the scrying mirror." Sephtis excitedly pulled the table over to Finnegan's body.

Voltaire nodded and left the laboratory. "Rune, can you bring the scrying mirror to Septhis?"

The tall mage nodded and started down the stairs.

"Rune told me about the choice before you." Leon looked uneasily at Voltaire.

"I chose Finnegan." Voltaire's voice was emotionless, but Leon's eyes and body relaxed.

Heading up the stairs, Voltaire knocked on K's door. "Come in," he heard Lilly calling from inside. "Lilly, Sephtis needs the crystal. And K, you should be by Finnegan's side when he wakes." Voltaire's voice was soft.

K's eyes widened. "What do you mean wakes up? You mean—" She rushed to Voltaire and hugged him, tears of elation streaming down her cheeks. "Thank you! Thank you! Oh gods, thank you, Voltaire!" She kissed him and rushed down the stairs.

Lilly stood and walked over to him, tears in her eyes. "It must have been a hard decision... I am sorry, Voltaire." She moved past him and placed a hand gently around his arm before heading to the laboratory.

Chapter 21

Inside everyone had already gathered and Sephtis was preparing the table. "Ah, Lilly, place the crystal on the top of the drawn triangle."

The young mage did as she was told and went to stand next to Leon and Rune. K was sitting right by Finnegan to help coax his spirit back.

"All right, let us begin." Sephtis started humming. It began softly, and the more he centered himself the deeper his tone became. This would be his greatest feat as a mage and he needed to be fully present. Walking up to the table that held a large book, he opened it slowly and began chanting the text, his voice thundering as he did so. After the first verse he lit a candle on the table. Sephtis continued chanting, moving to the other tables, and lighting the candles.

Voltaire stood alone, his heart still heavy.

The room steadily darkened and Sephtis's voice began to rise now that all the candles were lit. The embers ignited, casting a warm, flickering glow through the room-its only source of light. The scrying mirror held the image of Finnegan provided by Rune, who had agreed to help, much to his own surprise. Lilly stood by the crystal ball watching as it began to glow brightly, becoming a conduit of power for Sephtis. The table shook and the air in the room became heavy and thick.

Lilly grabbed Leon, who held onto Rune, and they watched in awe and fear as they began to feel something tearing. It felt wrong in a way, but Sephtis didn't stop and finally there was a sound of lightning. Then an explosion sent everyone flying into the walls and a dead silence fell around them.

"He's breathing!" K yelled and Finnegan started to cough as he sat up.

"What... What in the hells happened?" he asked shakily. The last thing he remembered was the agony he felt from his torn leg, but when he looked down it was all healed and he felt better than he ever had.

"Oh, thank the gods!" K grabbed Finnegan, kissing his face and lips. "You are never allowed to leave me again!"

Everyone let out their held breaths. So far, so good. But before anyone could get a word in, there was a thunderous boom and a man in long robes appeared in the room. He glowed unnaturally and his black eyes fixated on Sephtis.

"YOU! YOU STOLE ONE OF MY SOULS!" His voice boomed so loud all the others had to cover their ears.

Sephtis stood strong. "I did. This boy did not deserve to die. He deserved to live!"

The eyes swept around and landed on Finnegan, then fixed on the body of the woman. "YOU PLANNED ON TWO SOULS!!"

"NO!" This time Voltaire stepped forward. "I let my wife go. She died a little less than a year ago. Finnegan died only this morning. He died helping me... If you wish to punish someone, punish me."

Lilly panicked and tried to get away from Leon, who held onto her tightly.

The spirit began to settle down. "There must be balance. For one to return to life, one must die."

"I understand." Voltaire said, about to step forward.

"Get back, you fool!" Sephtis hissed, turning around to Voltaire. "You are still young, you have a life, a new one with friends and one who loves you, your children to live for. I have lived a long life... I have done the one thing I have spent the last fifty years working toward. I am tired... I wish to see my family." He turned back to the massive spirit in front of him. Sephtis felt no shame in what he had done. But he also understood there would be consequences for his actions. "Perhaps it is too much to ask, but may I say my goodbyes, spirit?"

The large black eyes fixated on him. As much as he detested what this fool mage had done, he couldn't help but admire his tenacity. "You may."

Sephtis turned to K. "Take care of yourself. You know what will happen upon my death. You were my daughter, K. Stay strong and remember all I taught you. This house and island now belong to you and Finnegan." He hugged her tight and kissed her forehead.

K started to cry. "Thank you...for everything."

Finnegan hugged Sephtis. "You old bastard... Here I thought you were going to go all dark side and what do you do? Prove me wrong... Thank you for being what K and I needed even though we didn't know it."

As they said their goodbyes, Voltaire heard his name. "Merrin..."

He spun around, and next to the glowing spirit stood the unmistakable image of Penelope. "Pen..." His heart caught in his throat, and he walked over to both of them.

She raised her hand, telling him not to come any closer.

"Pen, I'm so sorry!"

"There is no reason to be sorry. You did nothing wrong. None of it was your fault—remember that. Live your life, Merrin. Love and be happy. Be who you were meant to be, not the man you became to please me." She smiled softly, seeing the surprise on his face. "Goodbye, Killian Voltaire."

"Goodbye, Pen," he murmured, and her visage disappeared.

Sephtis stopped in front of Voltaire. "Well, my friend, it has been my greatest pleasure to have known you..." Sephtis hugged Voltaire tightly. "Take care of them. They need you."

"I promise, my friend, I will..." Voltaire returned the embrace. "I will see you again when the time comes."

"That will be in many, many years, I hope," Sephtis sighed and turned to meet his fate. "Thank you, spirit."

"Yes, it is time." The spirit stepped forward.

The last thing they heard Sephtis say before his body collapsed was "I see my family."

K wept and then cried out in pain as she grabbed her shoulder.

"What is it?" Finnegan asked with alarm. "What's wrong?" Seeing her shirt smoking, he tore it off. "Oh, gods..."

There, branded on K's shoulder, were two Ks in a circle.

Leon and Lilly looked confused and Rune's eyes widened. "King Killer...you...you were the one who killed the king!"

Finnegan wrapped his arm protectively around K. "I am sure she had good reason," he growled.

"Let's deal with this later..." Voltaire said. "Let's bury Sephtis and Penelope."

Everyone quickly turned toward Voltaire, nodded, and voiced their agreement.

"Ladies, can you get the men to start digging graves?" Voltaire asked.

"Of course." Lilly and K left and the men lifted up Sephtis, who had a small smile on his lips.

"Well, at least he died seeing his family again," Leon said softly.

"I hope the spirit won't punish him for what he did," Rune mused.

"I think it was satisfied with his soul," Voltaire said, helping the men pick him up. They carried him outside and returned to get Penelope.

The sailors had dug two graves next to the other five graves in which members of Septhis's family had been laid to rest. In silence they buried the two bodies. Some sailors spoke a few words. Others stayed silent.

As the sailors left the grieving friends, K stared at the mound of dirt. All these years the old man had kept her hidden. Kept her safe from the prying eyes of those who had hunted her. K's shoulder throbbed and she winced in pain.

The motion did not go unnoticed.

"Let's head inside, everyone," Voltaire said, motioning for the others to follow him. They moved without a word, making no sound other than that of their footsteps as they followed their captain to the study. Voltaire stopped at the liquor cabinet, pulled out crystal drinking glasses, and set them on the table. Then, grabbing Sephtis's finest whiskey, he poured everyone a drink.

Everyone fell silent, lost in their thoughts. Finnegan felt a mix of happiness and sadness. K was scared, Rune felt lost and frustrated, Leon was unsure, and Lilly... Lilly just seemed calm and ready to help anyone who needed it.

"So, our friend is gone, and though I grieve for him, I have something I must do," said Voltaire. "I must find my children..." He looked at the others and they all nodded in agreement. "But there is something else we need to deal with." He turned to K. "My friend...now is the time."

K looked at Voltaire and took in a shaky breath. He was right—now was the time. Taking another breath, she felt Finnegan's strong hand holding onto hers. Smiling appreciatively, she started her tale.

"I come from a noble family in Ahris, though not as high as Sephtis or even Finn... But my family was proud and they hosted the King and his Queen when I was fourteen. He had yet to have a child with his wife, so he was looking for concubines. I was the eldest daughter in the family and though I did not know it, at the time he was looking at me..."

Her voice trailed for a moment. "It was such a grand party. He even danced with me. I had been so excited; the King danced with me; it was such an honor. But I did not know what that dance would lead to. I was fifteen when I had my first blood and it was then I was packed up and sent away from my family to live in the palace. I didn't understand why. My mother said it was to help the Queen, though I had no idea how I could help a Queen." K's fingers started tapping, showing her growing agitation. Glancing around the table, she saw everyone raptly listening to her tale.

"Go on, love," Finnegan encouraged, knowing this was something she needed to get off her chest—something she had been holding in for far too long.

"Yes. I was given my own room and the King would visit me from time to time. He would bring me flowers, jewelry. I had beautiful clothes, but everything felt...wrong. I would often hear him yelling at the maids...I could hear their screams when he took them violently..." Tears threatened to break and her lips trembled. "It was a servant, Twila, an older woman who was looking out for me, who told me what I was there for. That my parents had sold me to the King for a higher position in the ranks of nobles... I was there to bear the King an heir, nothing more..."

Her jaw flexed as she grit her teeth. "A noble broodmare... I was terrified... All I could think was that he was going to do to me what he had done to those poor serving girls. I tried to escape but was only brought back by the soldiers. The King was so angry, but Twila, she was able to soothe his anger before he took it out on me. He had made a promise to keep away from me till I was older, till I could understand better. But one night the King had— Had too much to drink. He stumbled into my room yelling at me to come to him...but I was too scared. I ran... He was throwing things around, breaking things. I grabbed a letter opener, held it toward him, and then he laughed and got angry..."

Her words became faster as her eyes moved in memory. "He rushed toward me. Then he tripped; he fell right on top of me... The small knife in my hand pierced his heart, killing him." Her shoulders sagged. "The soldiers heard him scream and they rushed in, pulling him off of me. They knew it had been an accident, but when a servant came she went to the Queen screaming. The Queen was enraged and wanted me punished, killed in front of everyone. So they dragged me to the dungeons, branded me, and shackled me to the wall to await public execution. It was Twila who rescued me...gave me enough gold and food to escape. I learned to survive in the rat holes, the streets—places where no sane man would go. Until I met Sephtis. He was able to hide the brand...to stop the men from looking...but now...now, it is back and I do not know if they will come for me."

"You will be safe, K, I swear it!" Finnegan vowed.

Voltaire tilted his head. "We will eliminate the threat against you, K, as we find my children."

"What is your name?" Lilly suddenly asked.

K's eyes widened. "I haven't told anyone my name... Only Sephtis knew."

"It's all right, you don't have to tell us," Leon said leaning back.

"No... It's all right with Sephtis gone... My name is..." She paused and looked at Finnegan. "Isabeau Key."

Finnegan smiled wide. "Isabeau... Such a lovely name. But if it's all right with you— I got used to calling you K."

"I don't mind at all," she said, leaning over and kissing his lips.

"What about you>" Lilly turned to the captain. "Shall you return to Merrin?"

Voltaire suddenly realized that having Lilly address him by Merrin felt no different from having her call him Voltaire. "I like the way Voltaire rolls off the tongue. I think I shall keep it."

Rune finally spoke. "Well, then, we have sort of a plan... I think tomorrow we shall come up with a path, but for now we drink. Except for K, baby and all!"

"Wait," Finnegan said and turned to K. "What?"

"I never got the chance to tell you..." K twisted her fingers a moment and bit her lips slightly. "I'm pregnant."

"I am going to be a father!" he cried as he took K in his arms, whirled her around, and kissed her passionately.

"Next thing you know, they will be wanting to get married," Leon teased.

"I do... I mean... Wait, I probably should have waited till you asked," K giggled.

"Well, then, let me ask right now!" Finnegan got down on one knee. "K, my sweet, naughty minx, grifter extraordinaire, thief of my heart, I cannot live without you. I love you. Marry me. Be my wife. Make me the happiest man."

"Ahhh, my noble pirate. Who is to say who stole whose heart first, my love? And you already know the answer. Yes, yes, I will marry you." She smiled, grabbed his face, and planted a kiss on his already opening mouth before he could say another word.

Cheers rang out from the crowd.

Voltaire stood. "A toast, then! To the new couple, may fortune favor you always. To Sephtis for his sacrifice, to new friends, new family!"

K raised her glass. "To finding your children, to giving Finnegan's brother his comeuppance, and to getting this brand off!"

The group cheered loudly, drank, and slammed their drinks on the table in unison.